TO SAVE THE REFUGE

MICHAEL GEORGE

STRATTON
—PRESS—
Publishing Life

To Save The Refuge
Copyright © 2020 **Michael George**

Stratton Press Publishing
831 N Tatnall Street Suite M #188,
Wilmington, DE 19801
www.stratton-press.com
1-888-323-7009

ISBN (Paperback): 978-1-64895-027-8
ISBN (Hardback): 978-1-64895-029-2
ISBN (Ebook): 978-1-64895-028-5

Printed in the United States of America

Books by Michael George

Horses Lemons And Pretty Girls
Finding Perry Gray
Of Rain Barrels And Bridges

The Refuge Series
Why A Refuge
Bridge To No Good
Grass Was Greener

This book is dedicated to two very special people

Mardi Lacher
For her special friendship and
four days that saved my life

Pat Alexander
My beautiful, sweetheart cousin
I remember it all

PROLOGUE

SKIP HALBERTSON WAS EXCITED AS he mounted his uncle's snowmobile. For the first time since he started school, he was making some friends. Doing so was difficult for him after spending his whole life in city schools and now finishing his last two years of high school in Kingsburg. In this part of Minnesota, people still considered where they lived to be rural, although the environment in the entire Kingsburg area was in the midst of rapid change, becoming more urban every day.

None of that mattered to Skip as he started out. All he could think of was that he'd been invited to go along for a trail ride with the most popular kids in school, kids who were all members of the most exclusive club there. The DRs. Only the members knew what the DRs really were. Most of the kids thought it stood for the Drag Runners because so much of the club had to do with riding trails at high speeds on machines. Snowmobiles in the winter, four-wheelers in the summer.

Skip was sure he would soon know though. The club members must like him if they invited him along for one of their runs, and if they liked him well enough, he was hoping they'd let him join. So it was with a great deal of anticipation that he left his uncle's small farm, the trail he followed lit by a nearly full moon.

He met the rest of the group at the edge of the Clayborne National Wildlife Refuge, on the shore of the recently created

Heritage Lake. The refuge lay to the north of the county road where they met and to the south was Heritage Preservation Minnesota, a huge resort still expanding but already a hugely successful enterprise. Those who invested in it in the early stages of its development had made unreal amounts of money. It was on their already vast array of trails that Skip thought they were going to take their midnight trail ride.

Instead, they headed north across Heritage Lake, deep into the refuge. Far into a wild land they were forbidden to be. Crossing the lake, they spread out, each person pushing their machine hard as they crossed. Because he was driving an older machine and because he wasn't as experienced a rider as the others, Skip reached the other side dead last, even running behind those carrying two people.

The others had grouped up when he reached them and were already heading deep into the woods along animal trails. They followed the trails until they reached a large meadow where a small herd of deer were yarded up for the winter. It was there that something unexpected happened to Skip.

Using only hand gestures, the leader of the group instructed the others what he wanted done. They split into two groups and moved slowly until they more or less surrounded the small herd of deer. The deer were limited to where and how far they could run because of the snow depth. The snowmobiles did not have that limitation. All of the deer, with the exception of a yearling doe, ran into the woods as far as possible. The yearling tried to cross the meadow.

Given the snow depth and the speed of the machines, the chase didn't last long, and in a short time, the exhausted yearling stood trapped, almost in the center of the meadow. The leader of the group of snowmobilers dismounted his machine, then motioned for Skip to join him. Sick at heart over what they were doing, Skip did as he was instructed.

"I thought," Skip said to the group's leader as he reached him, "we were going on a trail ride. Why are we doing this?"

"Because, you idiot, we're the DRs."

"I don't think I know what you mean."

"Damn it, but you are stupid. We are the DRs. The Deer Runners, twit. Now, if you want to be a member of our club, what you got to do is kill that deer."

"I don't have a gun or nothin'," Skip argued.

"Don't matter. We don't use guns." The leader, an older man with a large gut, pulled a knife from a sheath on his belt. "Use this," he said, handing Skip the knife.

Skip just stood there, his hands hanging at his sides, refusing the knife. He looked around at the group and their smiling faces and knew without a doubt that he hadn't been invited along as an act of friendship. Only one person in the group didn't show her ridicule. She kept her helmet on and the protective face mask down, so Skip couldn't see her face.

"I think I'll just go home," Skip said to the leader and turned back toward his snowmobile.

"I don't think so," the leader said, motioning to the group to join him.

Before Skip reached his machine, two of the biggest boys in the group grabbed him. They held him as the leader slit the throat of the yearling deer, then proceeded to gut it while four of the other boys each held a leg of the dying deer, to keep their leader out of harm's way.

As the blood and intestines of the dying deer spilled out onto the white snow, the boys dragged Skip over to it, knocked him down, and pushed his face into the bloody mess. Someone kicked him in the ribs, and laughing, they left him lying there, next to the now dead animal. Only the girl with her helmet on stood back and didn't appear to laugh.

Coughing and trying to wipe the mess off his face, Skip wondered who she was. She was the only one, at that moment, that he didn't want to kill. The rest of them, he promised himself, he would get even with. One way or the other, he'd prove to everyone that he could do something really big.

He waited, lying there on the bloody snow, until they loaded the deer they so bravely slaughtered and left the refuge. When all sounds of their machines were out of his hearing, he slowly got to his feet, mounted his uncle's machine, and started toward home, his heart filled with the greatest hatred he'd ever known.

He had already seen more than his share of wrong, of evil, in his young life, but this was the basest cruelty of all.

They would pay for it though; somehow, they would all pay for it.

CHAPTER 1

ACK THOMAS WAS FREQUENTLY HAUNTED by the world around him. Many of the people he knew were recently murdered or hurt. First his wife, Julie, was killed when he was the real target. A year later, his fiancée, Mandy, a woman he'd known most of his life, was killed. A woman he barely knew yet that he felt as if he wasn't already in love with when she died, given enough time, he would have been. Many others in his life were hurt in other ways. From being shot in the head, to being kidnapped and raped, to things as simple as losing their jobs only because they in one way or the other helped him, or in some cases, only because they knew him.

The earth itself, in his part of Minnesota, was also being raped and destroyed by a large corporation building and rapidly expanding a resort called Heritage Preservation Minnesota. Most of it was on a large portion of what once was a national wildlife refuge. The rest was on all the formally private land around the refuge that they could gobble up.

This morning was one of Mack's bad times. He woke up in the small hours and wasn't able to fall back to sleep. Along with all the things already bothering him, this was the day he had a meeting with the president of the local bank. A bank owned by Land's Magnificent, the corporation responsible for the resort he totally despised.

Even though Mack had a great deal of respect for the bank president, Harley Anderson, he had little interest in whatever it was the man wanted to talk to him about. Mack would have declined to go to any meeting dealing with the bank had anyone else asked him to come. He very likely would have told Harley Anderson no too, if the man hadn't insisted that it was extremely important. That it was important to Mack and to those he cared about. So Mack relented and agreed to go, provided the meeting was the first thing in the morning so it didn't interfere with his work day.

Mack was a Clayborne County Deputy Sheriff, and with the department so woefully understaffed, he wanted to be out and about most of the day where he was needed.

Mack was up, dressed, and drinking a much needed cup of coffee when his father, Ben, joined him in the kitchen of the townhouse they shared.

"What are you doing up at this hour, Mack?" Ben asked him. "You having those bad dreams again?"

"No, no dreams, Dad. I just couldn't sleep. Too much on my mind, I guess."

"Seems like, to me anyway, you've always got too much on your mind. What is it this time? That meeting with Harley bothering you?"

"Some. That and all the crap going on around here."

"Like which crap this time?"

"You know, Dad. The constant crime of all kinds that we've had since the resort was started, not to mention the poaching and totally senseless slaughter of nearly every kind of critter there is out in the refuge. More than that though, I'm worried about Lisa Anderson and the rest of her family. They're having a hard time of it, with Margaret still in the hospital."

"Is there anything I can do?"

"Not right now. I'm helping Lisa deal with what happened to her. Beth is a lot of help too. Lisa's a strong kid, so I think she'll be okay in time. It takes a lot of time though, to get over the way she was so brutally beaten and raped."

"It doesn't mean there isn't anything I can do. If nothing else, I can help with their medical bills. It's better I spend my money that way than on the kind of junk most of the world's idiots spend their money on."

"Yeah, you're right. Wait though, until we have a better idea of what they need. And don't plan on giving all your money away. I've got enough to worry about, without having to worry about you too."

"It's a damn truth that you don't need more to worry about, given how you constantly take the weight of the whole world on your shoulders." Ben sighed, then shook his as if he was trying to rid Mack of his troubles. "Enough of that. As long as we're up, can I make you some breakfast?"

"Not right now. I think I'll take a run over to the refuge, see if there are any critters out and about. I think I'll feel better if I get out amongst some real life for a bit. If I get back early enough, you can make breakfast then. If not, I'll grab a bite later, when I meet Dale at Katie's Kafe."

"Okay, and if I don't see you, tell Mister Sheriff Dale Magee hello for me. He's a good man, Sheriff Magee is. It does my heart good to see what good friends you two are."

"Mine too," Mack agreed with a smile. "I think I'll get going now. I'm kind of anxious to get out there."

"Yeah, I know. I also know that the critters you're looking for are the mostly the two-legged kind. I ain't so old that I don't know how bad you want to do something about the poaching going on. So while you're out there, be damn careful. The one thing I don't need is you taking any more bullets," Ben said, referring to the time Mack was shot right after he started the deputy sheriff's job.

"They were shotgun pellets, Dad."

"Either way, they can make you just as dead. So be careful."

Mack sighed. "I will, Dad."

Mack drove directly to the new bridge, built on a main county road to accommodate Heritage Lake, which was created by damming the Saint Catherine River running through the Clayborne National Wildlife Refuge. It also was needed now to accommodate the vastly increased traffic loads.

He stopped in the middle of the bridge and stood watching the full moon cast blue-gray shadows on the rippling snow covering the vast expanse of the lake. It should have been a silent place so early in the morning and would have been if snowmobiles weren't running through the wooded land on the other side. The only other sound was the soft purr of his four-wheel drive pickup, parked next to him.

He waited for the sound he knew would come, yet when he heard the sharp crack of the high-powered rifle, it startled him.

He quickly got into his truck, drove to the end of the bridge, and down the ramp used for launching boats in the summer. He drove without lights, letting the moon guide him as he raced across the snow-covered ice, using the trails made by the hated snowmobiles he was looking for.

They weren't hard to find. Mack Thomas knew the Clayborne National Wildlife Refuge well, after spending most of his life living next to it. He knew where the deer would be yarded in that area and knew that the men on the snowmobiles who had fired the rifle were after the deer.

He left the truck at the edge of the lake, and moving slowly, almost silently along the trail, he moved up on the two men bent over the body of a deer.

Mack took them completely by surprise. They were so intent on gutting the big buck they'd just slaughtered, they didn't know he was there until they heard him inject a shell into the twelve-gauge pump shotgun he carried.

"You ain't got no jurisdiction here, Thomas," one of the men complained when they recognized Mack.

"Not as a deputy sheriff," Mack answered. "There's nothing that says I can't make a citizen's arrest."

"You fuck wit' us," the second man said, "an' you'll for sure regret it."

"You bet. Now get on your feet. You're going to drag that deer over to the lake and load it on my truck. It's evidence."

"Hey, asshole, this sucker's heavy. We'll haul it over there on the machines."

"No, you'll drag it."

Reluctantly, the two killers started to drag the deer. As soon as they were a safe distance from the snowmobiles, Mack turned his back to them and fired twice. The pellets from his twelve-gauge penetrated the fuel tanks at that close range, and both machines burst into flames.

"Hey, you asshole," the bigger of the two poachers yelled, "you can't do that!"

"I already did," Mack answered with a smile. "That's what happens when you try to escape. You don't like it, stop poaching deer."

"Von Herter ain't gonna like it that you done it. Thems was his machines."

The poacher was referring to Eric Von Herter, Clayborne County's richest man. A supposedly respected businessman. Mack knew, though, that he was the man who controlled most of the drug traffic in Clayborne County and the surrounding area. A man Mack Thomas hated with all his soul.

"I think you be a dead man now, Thomas," the poacher threatened.

"And I think it's time for you to shut your mouth," Mack countered. "Or you might be the dead man."

The poacher opened his mouth to answer Mack, then caught the look in his eyes. He shut it.

After the deer was loaded on the bed of his pickup, Mack told the poachers to get on the back with it and handcuffed both men to the tie downs on the sides of it, as close to the deer as he could get them. He knew that by the time he got them to jail, they would be well bloodied by the deer carcass. He wanted them that way. He also knew that given the way they were sweating from dragging the dead deer, they would both be well chilled by the frigid Minnesota night air long before he got them there. At the current temperature, the cover on the back of Mack's pickup wasn't going to do much to keep them warm.

On his way, Mack called his friend, Rich Hayden, who was the manager of the refuge, and told him what had happened. Rich agreed to check out the site of the killing, then to meet Mack at the jail. He didn't have any more time or patience for poachers than Mack did.

The poachers were shaking hard from the cold when they reached the sheriff's office. Mack took them off the bed of his truck one at a time, cuffing their hands behind them as he did. Then, his shotgun at the ready, he marched them into the booking area and turned them over to the deputy on duty after explaining their crime.

The deputy was smiling when Mack finished. There were no deputies working for Sheriff Dale Magee who had any tolerance for the kind of men Mack brought in. Nor did they have any for Eric Von Herter, the man they considered the scourge of Clayborne County, if not all of Minnesota.

Rich Hayden, the manager of the refuge arrived at the sheriff's office shortly after Mack did, his face carrying a sly smile.

"What happened, Mack?" he asked. "Did those machines try to attack you?" He laughed.

"Naw," Mack answered, "I was alone when I caught the poachers and there were two of them and only one of me, so I was worried they'd escape. I did the only safe thing I could do and cut off their means to do so."

Rich laughed even harder. "I think, Mack, that was probably the most prudent thing you could have done." His laughter continued as he slapped Mack across the back, obviously pleased with Mack's method of dealing with the men.

"So," Mack asked, "are we going to throw the book at those two?"

"You damn right. The book and anything else I can get my hands on. Like you, I've had enough of this kind of crap. And thanks, Mack, for having the balls to do something about it. I don't know why you were out there at this hour of the morning and I don't care. I just wish I could have you, or someone like you, out there all night, every night."

"Me too," Mack agreed

CHAPTER 2

Mack entered the Kingsburg State Bank with a feeling of dread. It didn't help any that he liked and respected Harley Anderson, the man he was meeting with. This was a bank and Harley was a banker. Mack preferred to avoid both.

As soon as Mack reached the reception desk in the lobby, the lady behind it stood and, without comment, led Mack to Harley's office. Harley shook Mack's hand, then motioned for him to sit down on the chair across from his desk.

"Mack," Harley said without any preliminaries, "if there was anyone else in the world sitting in that chair, I'd be telling them that I have some great news for them. Given it's you sitting there, I'm sure what I have to tell you today is a mixed bag."

"I don't mean to be rude, Harley, but could you just tell me what the hell this is about? I've got a meeting with Dale in about a half hour. He's real busy, as you know, so I hate to keep him waiting."

"Don't worry about that, Mack, I've already talked to Dale. You can give him a call when we're done here. He'll meet with you then."

"What exactly is this about, that it's going to take so long?"

"It's about the rest of your life, Mack, that's what it's about. Before we go any farther with this meeting, I have a question. And before I ask it, I have to tell you, I'm only asking because I want to know, not because I need to know."

"That's fine with me, Harley," Mack sighed, letting his impatient show. "Only, can we get on with this. I'd like to get whatever it is over with. I'm pretty sure now that I'm not going to like what you're going to tell me."

"Like I said, anyone else, it would be incredibly good news. Only with you is it possible that news like this be a mixture of good and bad. My question is this, how much did you know about Mandy and Jason's finances?"

His question referred to Mack's murdered fiancée and her estranged husband, who disappeared on the same day she was murdered.

"I sure don't know why you're asking me that. Since it's you asking, I'll answer it. Damn little. All I know for sure is that Mandy was the one who paid their household expenses. Jason was supposedly handling their investments. Trouble was, he wouldn't tell Mandy what he was doing. And I know that near the end, she was trying to figure out what he was doing. I know she got into his computer at least once, maybe more. That's it. I don't know anything else for sure. I suspect, though, that he probably spent a fair amount of his income on his ladies. Jason always did like the ladies."

Harley smiled at Mack's comments about Jason's ladies.

"Well, you're wrong about how he spent his money," he said, still smiling. "He was too cheap, I think, to spend much on anyone other than himself. He did, however, invest a lot of money. An incredible amount more than he made here at the bank."

"So what has any of that got to do with me?" Mack's impatience was becoming more than just obvious.

"I'm getting to that, Mack. First, let me tell you what happened. After Mandy died, Wanda Peterson, now Wanda Thomas, your uncle's wife, found some computer disks while she was packing Mandy's things for you. They were in a rather large envelope with my name on it, so she gave them to Dale, who brought them to me. Those disks had all of Jason's financial records on them."

"I still don't see what that's got to do with me?"

"Please try to have some patience, Mack," Harley said, showing some frustration with Mack. "After what I've been through to get us where we are today, you will hear me out. Jason didn't want anyone to know what he was doing, especially not Mandy. The records on the disks were for the most part written in various codes of Jason's creation and were purposely recorded in a way that initially made little to no sense. Add to that, Jason was too cheap to upgrade his computer. The programs he was using were all written so long ago and so out of date that I had one hell of a time finding a way to work with them."

"Harley, please get to it. I don't know much at all about computers, so you're talking a foreign language here. Can you maybe skip the technical garble and just tell me what this is about?"

"Yeah, well, sure, save to say, I got a couple of hackers—"

"Computer guys, right?"

"Yes, Mack, computer guys. Anyway, Jason got his hands on a lot of money, moved it around fast, then invested nearly all of it in one company. That money has made a lot more money."

"I still don't see what any of this has to do with me."

"It has everything to do with you. In order to cover his probably illegal activities, Jason put nearly everything in Mandy's name. He wasn't too bright, thinking he'd get away with anything that way, but that's what he did. And as for his illegal activities, that's the one thing I haven't been able to figure out. He covered his tracks well."

"So what. It still doesn't have anything to do with me."

"It does, Mack. Mandy also had a will done after she left Jason. She left everything to you."

"You're kidding! Why would she do that? I didn't want her money."

"Maybe not, Mack. She, however, evidently loved you deeply and wanted you to have what she had if anything happened to her. So the deal is, you've just inherited a fair amount of money. A lot more money than she could have possibly suspected she had."

"This is totally nuts. I didn't…don't want her money. Especially not if it came from Jason."

"Before you go refusing it, Mack, think about the good you can do with it. There are countless good things you can do."

"Harley, you know I don't really care much about money, so how can I take this, no matter what the amount is? I never did anything to earn it."

"I have a better question. How can you not take it? It's like this, Mack, if you don't accept it, the money will sit in this bank, making money for this bank, while a lot of people you don't like fight over it. In the end, a good part of it will end up making some already rich attorneys richer. If that's what you want to happen to something Mandy wanted you to have, then go right the hell and refuse it."

"Harley, you sure are making this difficult."

Harley smiled. "Yes, I am. And it's not an accident that I am. I know you too well to not have prepared for this meeting. I've given this a lot of thought, and I very much want you to take this money and do some good with it. It's well past time some good came of all the bad things Jason did in his life. We both know too that this is definitely what Mandy wanted."

"You're probably right, Harley. Trouble is, what kind of good can I do with it? I've never even considered having money, so I've never thought much about what I'd do with it if I did have it."

"If you think about it, I'm sure you'll come up with a lot of things you can do with it. You've got a lot of friends who could use some help, Bob Anderson especially. The sheriff's department could use new computers, a few new cars, etc., and that's just a small start. There are environmental organizations, the local food shelf, and the list goes on. There's just no telling the good you can do."

"You've already named a lot of ways to spend the money. So tell me, since you mentioned so many ways to spend it, just how much money are we talking about here?"

"The stock alone is in the multiple eight figures."

"How much?"

"Many millions. Like I said, Jason bought a lot of stock in one company while it was still relatively low. That stock has since gone way up. The early shares he bought have gone up six, seven times what he paid for them. Everything he bought has, at minimum, doubled. So it amounts to millions. I'd have to get the current numbers from today's market to tell you exactly how much."

"What stock is it?"

"Land's Magnificent. Like I said, there are some other stocks, bonds, and other things, but the bulk of it is Land's Magnificent stock."

"Well, Harley, I don't know if you emphasized that stock to convince me to accept the money or if you told me about it to tell me what a great deal owning it is, but you did convince me. I will accept the money because you're right, there are some things I can do with it. Before we get into that, are you willing to help me handle it? I don't know anything about how to deal with it, and I also don't want anyone to know where the money is coming from if I do help them. You know, of course, that I'm willing to pay you whatever it is you want to charge me for your services."

Harley smiled, then laughed. "Of course, Mack, I'll be more than glad to help you. That includes taking care of the taxes you're going to have to pay. And as for my charging you for it, there's no problem there. In fact, you already owe me near a hundred thousand for the work I've already done for you. I've been more than glad to help you with this, but I'm way too much of a banker to have done it for nothing when there's this kind of money involved. Besides, I'm going to retire soon. The money you already owe me and the money you will be paying me is going to make that retirement a lot better. Maybe even buy me the RV the missus and I have been talking about for a while now."

"Good, you've earned both." This time, Mack smiled. "Now, the first thing I want you to do is sell all, and I mean all, of that damn stock. Then figure out a decent, safe place to put the money. Just make sure a lot of it goes somewhere that I can spend it if I want to. I don't want too much of it tied up somewhere that I can't get at it. There's too much to do."

"I was afraid you wouldn't like the stock thing. I'll sell it for you, only not until I tell you that there's nothing else out there that will make you the kind of money it will."

"I don't care. You know how much I hate what that company is doing to the refuge, so I surely don't want anything to do with it. Not one damn thing! Now, the next thing I want you to do is deposit about fifty thousand in Bob Anderson's checking account, then find out every bill and he and his family have and pay them. And you're going to do it in a way that he doesn't know who's supplying the money, and as important, do it so he can't find out. You also have to agree to never tell anyone about any of this. Not the money and not what I'm doing with it. Those few that I want to know about it, I'll tell them. Can you do all that? And can you start today? Especially with the Andersons?"

"Yes, Mack, I can do that. Anything else?"

"Oh yes, but you'd better start writing. I've got a long list."

Harley smiled again. "Before we do that, there's someone I want you to meet. I think he will have some good ideas for you on how to invest some of the money. Do you mind meeting him?"

"Who is he? Another banker?"

"No, Mack, he's my son. He makes his living as a defense attorney. And before you get upset about that, I have to tell you, he's an ardent environmentalist, with some strong ideas on how not to simply save it, but also to improve it."

"Will this take long?"

"Only as long as you want it to."

"Okay, Harley, because he's your son, I'll talk to him."

"Good, give me a minute." Harley left the room and quickly returned with his son. "Mack," he said, "this is my son, Kalif Anderson."

Kalif held out his hand and Mack stood to shake it. "It's nice to finally meet you, Mack," he said. "I've heard a lot about you."

"Mostly bad, I'd guess," Mack answered.

"Quite the contrary. There are, believe it or not, a lot of people that admire you."

"Mack," Harley said, "You two have a lot to talk about. Most of which, I don't need to hear. So I'll be close by when you're done. You and I, Mack, can finish up what you want done then."

"I don't know the details of your current situation, Mack," Kalif said as soon as Harley was out of the room. "Dad is too conscientious to tell me very much. He did tell me how you feel about what's going on in this county, your concern about the environment, and the fact that you have come into a fair amount of money. I'm here to tell you what I'm up to, and how I and some other concerned individuals think we can turn some of this around."

"It's too late for the refuge, isn't it? If it can't be saved, how much good can we do? Can anyone actually do any good?"

"I think so. None of us can save the world. We can, however, do some real good, make some positive changes, and maybe set some good examples for other places, if those of us who care try to work together."

"That all sounds good. The trouble is, I haven't seen anything like that happening. Not here, not anywhere."

"I know. Will you give me the time to explain what I have in mind?'

"If it doesn't take too long. There are a lot of problems out there I should be taking care of right now. They're important too."

"I understand, Mack. I have a busy practice, which is right now demanding my attention. I have a lot of clients, both guilty and innocent, who need my defense. I think this is just as, if not more, important."

"Okay," Mack agreed with a heavy sigh, "explain away."

It was another two hours before Mack left the bank.

CHAPTER 3

SHERIFF DALE MAGEE WAS WAITING for Mack when he walked
into Katie's Kafe, located on the main street of Kingsburg,
just two short blocks from the Kingsburg National Bank. It
was close to the noon hour now, so the place was already nearly filled
with the lunch crowd.

"Sorry it took so long, Dale," Mack said as he sat down. "There
was a lot more to that meeting than I could have ever imagined."

"I don't care about that, Mack. Shit happens. What I am a bit
concerned about now are the events you were involved in early this
morning."

"Why? It's perfectly legal for me to arrest poachers. Any citizen
has that right."

"Sure, but why the hell did you have to destroy those machines?
One way or the other, at best, someone is going to end up paying
for them. Given the kind of money you make, it's going to be the
department."

"No, it's not. There's no way anyone is paying Von Herter for
those machines."

"There's no way out of it, Mack. First Von Herter called, screaming as usual, then his lawyer called. The department is already over
budget, so there's no way we can afford to fight it."

"The department isn't going to have to. It's all being taken care
of as we speak. If Von Herter wants to get paid for snowmobiles he

lends out to poachers, it's going to cost him more than a couple of hundred new machines would." Mack smiled, letting Dale know that he was going to enjoy doing it too. "That goes for any future poachers I catch. From now on, one way or the other, I am going to destroy every single one of their snowmobiles. For that matter, any machines they're using when I catch them."

"How do you figure we aren't going to have to pay for the two you destroyed this morning? And if you do it again, it could get real expensive. I just told you, we can't afford to fight it, not to mention you pulling this crap again."

"And as I just told you, Dale, the department doesn't have to pay for it. You don't even have to worry about it. So don't."

"Just how are we not going to have to pay for them? And when you get wild ideas like you have now, what can I do except worry?"

"There's more than one reason why nothing's going to be done about it. The main reason being that Von Herter can't afford to fight us right now. Not with what it will cost him to do it if he tries. One of the things I learned this morning is, the man is having some serious cash flow problems."

"He still has attorneys on retainer. We don't."

"Well, like I said, even that's being taken care of. One of the things you're forgetting is that when Von Herter let those guys use his machines to poach, it made him an accessory. He pushes, and he will be arrested for poaching. Rich Hayden and I will both be pressing charges against him if he so much as mentions it again. After that, anything that happens in the refuge that shouldn't happen, I'll arrest him again. So quit worrying about it. We've got a lot more important things to talk about right now."

"Sure we do," Dale said, then argued, "You're still going to have to stop doing things the way you did this morning. I know you take it personal when people start poaching and otherwise raising hell out there in the refuge, what's left of it anyway. You just can't be going around destroying property that way just because you're pissed."

"Dale, I just told you what I'm going to be doing, and I wasn't kidding," Mack said, using a tone of voice that told Dale that he for sure wasn't kidding. "So let's get to something that really matters. We still need a trained detective to help me with the more difficult cases. As soon as possible, I want to find one we can use as a consultant when I need help. The way things are going, there's no doubt I'll be needing it."

"I just told you, the department is over budget, and now you want to hire a detective as a consultant. Hell, Mack, if you weren't working at half pay, you wouldn't even be a deputy. The sheriff's department would be limping along without any kind of detective, not to mention one as good as you are."

Mack laughed. "You know, Dale, you could ask me what my meeting with Harley was about this morning. Aren't you curious?"

"I haven't thought about it. I figured your latest stunt was more important. More of a problem anyway."

"It's not a problem. So now do you want to hear about my meeting or not. And by the way, the department is going to get enough up-to-date cell phones for every deputy, three new squad cars, and a new computer system. The new one is supposed to be simple enough so even I can use it."

"What are you talking about, Mack? Are you using or something? You aren't making any sense at all. A consultant detective, cell phones, new cars, and a new computer system. You're not making any sense. None at all."

"I know, Dale. I'm not making any sense. I'm not trying to. And until you quit with your side of this conversation, I'm not going to. My question is, do you or don't you want to know what happened in the meeting I had with Harley?"

"I guess I don't have a choice. It sure doesn't look like I'm going to get anything sensible out of you until you tell me."

"That's right, you won't. But before I tell you, you've got to promise me that what I tell you will be kept in the strictest confidence. You don't tell anyone, not even Kathy," Mack said, referring to Dale's fiancée.

"Now you have got me curious. And yes, I won't repeat whatever it is you have to tell me."

"Good. Now this is what happened…"

Mack went on to tell Dale about the meeting he had with Harley Anderson, the bank president, everything about it except his conversation with Kalif Anderson and where some of the money was already going. The part about where the rest of the money was going, he had no intention of telling anyone. What he'd done with it was done only because to him it was the right thing to do. It wasn't done for thanks or glory.

"Jesus, Mack," Dale said, a look of disbelief on his face, "that's wild. Did you really actually order three new squad cars and a new computer system for the department?"

"No, I didn't actually do it myself. Harley's taking care of it for me. The department will be getting them though, as soon as it can be arranged."

"Be damned, we sure do need them."

"Yes, and we will be hiring a new detective consultant too."

"How the hell are you going to manage that? Giving the department new equipment is one thing, hiring a detective, even just as a consultant, I don't know…"

"Harley's setting that up too. And I have someone in mind. Is it okay with you with you if I talk to him?"

"Who is it you have in mind?"

"Paul Danielson, the cop in Minneapolis who helped me out when Lisa Anderson was kidnapped. He's a good man. Intelligent too."

"I don't see why not. You're the one paying the bill. I would like to talk to him, though, before we make it official."

"Good enough, I'll give him a call tonight. Set up a meeting. With the three of us, if you want."

"No, you talk to him first. If he's interested, then the three of us will get to—"

Dale's comments were interrupted by his cell phone. "Oh damn," he said after answering it. "Mack and I will be right there."

"What's up, Dale?" Mack asked.

"Someone's been found dead in that piece of crap motel north of town. Looks like murder."

"Not another kid, I hope," Mack said, referring to two boys murdered the previous year.

"No. This one is an adult male with a knife wound. We'd best roll. I'll meet you there."

CHAPTER 4

THE MOTEL WAS IN OBVIOUS need of repair. The paint on the clapboard siding was peeling, the fascia board was beginning to rot away, and the roof looked as if it would take a miracle for it to keep the place dry inside. The small room Mack walked into carried a distinct musty, dirty smell, even with the strong odor of blood that permeated it.

The nude body of a middle-aged man lay on its back, nearly surrounded by blood, with a large hunting knife stuck in its open mouth, coming out the back of its throat.

Mack instantly felt his stomach turn. Dale's face quickly developed a distinctly green tinge to it.

"It doesn't take any more than a quick look," Dale said, "to know this is a bad one."

"No, it sure doesn't," Mack agreed. "Given where he was stabbed and as deep as the knife went in, it obviously was done intentionally. I wonder what kind of a total nut case we're up against this time."

"I don't know, Mack. It does look like that's who, or should I say what, did this."

"So who found the body?"

"The owner of this dump. I guess he found it when he came in to clean the room this morning."

"Clean hell. This place doesn't look like it's been cleaned for a long time. If it's okay with you, Dale, I think I'll go have a little talk with him. See if I can find out who this guy was with."

"Good idea, Mack. I'll see to it that things are taken care of here. Try to keep things reasonably decent for the medical examiner. I sure wish we had access to a decent forensic team."

"So do I. Do you think we could get a team or at least someone from Minneapolis or Hennepin County to give us some help? Maybe you ought to give them a call, see if they can."

"Mack, you know we can't afford—"

Mack gave Dale a grim smile. "I can, Dale, so try."

"Okay, this time. We're going to have to talk about all this later. I'm not going to have you paying for all of Clayborne County's law enforcement."

"Sure, later. Right now, I'm going to find out what I can from the guy who owns this dump while you keep an eye on things and make some calls on your wonderful cell phone. If I didn't understand the use we have for them, I sure as hell wouldn't want one myself."

Feeling guilty for walking out on Dale yet grateful that he could, Mack left the stench of the room. He found the motel's owner sitting in a ragged overstuffed chair in his office, a newspaper in his lap and a fat smelly cigar smoldering in his mouth. His chin was stained yellow from the saliva dripping off the cigar.

"What can I do for you?" he asked Mack as he slowly lifted his pudgy face from his newspaper.

Mack showed his badge to the man. "For starters, you can tell me who rented the room with the body in it."

"The one on the bed rented it."

"Do you know who he was with?"

"No, I surely don't. He parked a ways away from the entrance, so I couldn't see who he was with. I can tell you one thing though, I damn well wish I had. Business has been bad enough without this kind of crap. Think you'll catch the bastard that done it to the man?"

"That's something we never know until we do. If you think of anything else, I'd appreciate if you'd give me a call." Mack gave the man his card. "That goes for anything you think of. It doesn't need to seem like it's something big."

"Sure, I can do that. Doubt like hell I'll think of anything though."

"Maybe not. Try anyway."

"Come to think of it," the motel man said, scratching his nearly bald head, "there was one thing. It probably don't mean much though."

"You never know, so what was the one thing?"

"The guy's jacket. It had a big DR on the back of it. Nothin' else, just a big DR. Oh, and the jacket was all black, except the sleeves. They was red. Wasn't nothin' else, just a big DR."

"Well, thanks," Mack said. "Maybe it isn't much, but it's something."

When he went back to the motel room, Mack looked around the room for the jacket without touching anything. It was apparently gone.

"I don't know if it means anything or not, Dale," he said. "The guy in the office said that when he checked in, the guy was wearing a jacket with a big DR on the back. Said it was black with red sleeves. It's not here. Not where I can see it anyway."

"Why it's not here, Mack, I don't know. I have seen some of the high school kids wearing them. Mostly, or maybe only, boys. Never gave it any thought before. I just figured it was just another club of some kind."

"It probably is. It might be a place to start looking though."

"It might be at that. I did look through the guy's pants for his identification. I'm going to have to notify his family today. He was carrying two driver's licenses. It wasn't hard to tell which one was a fake."

"Yeah, the guy told me he looked at the guy's ID. He probably didn't care if it was real or not. Anything for a buck."

"Well, we can talk to him more about it later. In the meantime, why don't you follow up on the DR thing? The guy's name is Gary Baldwin. I think he was one of the construction workers over at the resort. I'll take care of notifying his family, if he has one." Dale paused a moment to gather his thoughts, then said, "You should start checking at the high school. Start with the administration, see if they know anything about the DR jacket thing. Then maybe talk to some of the kids. I don't think you should tell any of the kids you talk to why you're asking them questions. We don't want to be upsetting any of them. Not until we're forced to and after the teachers and administration at the school are at least somewhat prepared to handle the situation if this has anything to do with that club or whatever it is."

"No, Dale, I won't. This is going to be tough enough to handle anyway. Do you think there was a chance this guy was a homosexual?"

"I have no idea. What's the reason for the question?"

"The way he was stabbed. It took someone fairly strong to drive the knife that deep. And what the hell was he doing with his mouth open the way it is? It just seems like the kind of killing a man would do. If he was straight, what was he doing here with a man?"

"I guess what you say makes sense. I hadn't even started to think along those lines. Do me a favor and be careful who you ask that question. This is still a small town, even if it is screwed up by that stinking resort and their big city crap. It would be devastating for the guy's family if a story like that got out. Even if it is true."

"Sure, Dale, I will do that. There's no sense in starting any unfounded rumors about a dead man. And you're right, his family is going to have enough to contend with as it is. I sure don't envy you, having to tell them."

"I'm not looking forward to it either."

"Well, I guess I'll get out and about, see if I can learn anything."

On his way to the high school, Mack used his cell phone to call Minneapolis Police Detective Paul Danielson. He answered on the second ring.

"Are you real busy?" Mack asked as soon as he did.

"Not so's you'd notice," Paul told him. "I'm taking a few days off. I've got a lot of vacation coming. The wife is at her mother's again. Pissed at me for working too much. So I thought I'd take a few days I could enjoy. Ain't likely I'd enjoy them that much if she was here. So what's up with you, Mack?"

"Actually a lot. I just left the scene of a murder. A man was found stabbed to death in a local motel. Knife went into his mouth and out the back of his throat. But that's not the main reason I called. The reason is, have you ever considered doing any consultant work? We really need a well-trained detective in the sheriff's department for me to work with, and I just got permission to talk to you about. You interested?"

"Hell, I don't know. I never gave doing something like that any thought. You said you guys were having budget problems up there and couldn't afford any more personnel. Isn't that why you're working at half pay? Or did something change so you can afford to hire someone as a consultant?"

"Yes, something changed. What do you think? Are you interested?"

"I just don't know, Mack, let me think on it some."

"While you're thinking on it some, as long as your wife is at her mother's, would you mind coming up here for a couple of days as a consultant to give me a hand with this murder. I've got a gut feeling that this is going to be a bad one. There's something about it that tells me that if we don't catch the killer quickly, it isn't going to stop with just one murder."

"Do you have any specific reasons for those feelings, Mack?"

"Yes, the way he was murdered. I doubt a knife in an open mouth is all that common. So why don't you take a drive to the country so we can talk it over? At least give me some hints on how to solve something like this."

"Now that sounds like a bit of a con, Mack," Paul said, then laughed. "What the hell, why not? Where and when should we meet?"

They agreed to meet the first thing in the morning at Katie's Kafe. Mack neglected to tell him that Dale would be there too and at the same time decided not to bother Dale with the fact Paul was coming. He didn't see any sense in making any of it too official, and he wanted the two men to meet without any anticipation on the part of either one of them.

Mack went directly to the principal's office when he got to the high school. A young lady with a big, if forced, smile greeted him from the other side of the reception desk.

"How can I help you, sir?" she asked, eyeing him up and down, curious, Mack was sure, about the Western style clothes he'd worn since he was a bull rider on the rodeo circuit.

Mack showed her his badge. "I'd like to see the principal, if it's at all possible," he told her.

"I take it this is something official," she said.

"It is."

"Well, Mr. Locks said he shouldn't be disturbed for a while, but I guess I could ask him if he'll see you, if it really is important?"

"Mr. Locks isn't Dan Locks, is it," Mack asked. "And, yes, it is important. Real important."

"Yes, Mr. Locks is Dan Locks, and yes, I will go ask him. May I give him your name, sir?"

"Mack Thomas. And you don't ever have to sir me. You see me again, Mack will do just fine."

Her public smile turned into a real one. "Okay, Mack, I'll go talk to Mr. Locks."

In less than a minute after she went into Dan Locks's office, he came out, his hand stretched out to meet Mack's.

"Let's talk in my office," Dan said, knowing from the grim look on Mack's face that he was there for something serious.

"I'm glad to see it's you here," Mack told him. "When did you get the promotion? Last time I saw you, you were still principal of the middle school."

"It's only supposed to be temporary. When Bradley Walters, the man who was the principal here, died of a heart attack just two days before school started, some moves had to be made in a hurry. So right now, I'm filling in here and my assistant principal at the middle school is filling in for me. So what brings you here, Mack? Nothing too serious, I hope. I'm going just a little bit nuts today already."

"What's driving you nuts today, Dan?"

"About an hour ago, I got a call, asking where the new computers were to be delivered. Twenty-five of them. State of the art yet.

Since we haven't ordered any new computers and can't afford new computers, I found the question a bit strange. So I've been trying to find out what's going on. The only thing I have been able to learn is that the computers do in fact belong to the school and that the middle school is getting twenty-five of them too. Who bought them and why is a mystery. No one seems to know. But that's my problem. I've got a sinking feeling that your problem is far more serious."

Mack had to force himself to keep from smiling because he was the one behind the new computers.

"It is, Dan," he answered after a moment's hesitation. "First, as I've done in the past, I've got to ask you not to tell anyone except those who really need to know, at least not today, what I'm going to tell you. We don't want this to get out until we, you, and everybody involved is prepared to handle it."

"Please don't tell me, Mack, that this is as serious as it was the last time you and I had a talk like this."

"It might be."

"Damn! Well, you've got my word, I'll keep everything as quiet as possible."

"Good. We've got another murder on our hands. A man was found in that northside motel. Stabbed to death. His name is Gary Baldwin."

"I don't think I know him. Why are you here about an adult who was murdered?"

"One of the few leads we have has to do with the jacket the guy was wearing. Do you know anything, Dan, about a club or something called DR? The man was supposedly wearing a jacket with the letters DR on it when he checked into that motel last night."

"Not much. I think the DR stands for Drag Runners. It's some kind of snowmobile club, I think. About all I know is that none of the kids who wear the jackets have ever been in any kind of serious official trouble. We tend to leave the kids' organizations and clubs alone as long as they aren't supported by school funds and don't make any trouble."

"Is it a very big club?"

"Not real big, I don't think. It's mostly made up of athletes. At least they're the boys I've noticed wearing the jackets. Beyond that, I don't think there's anything I can tell you."

"Well, I appreciate your taking the time to talk to me anyway. All too many people in your position aren't willing to bother."

"Mack, after those boys were killed and you handled the whole thing so well even though you were a total rookie then, you'll always have my time. But tell me, how is the job going? You still like it?"

"Yes and no. It's satisfying to feel like I'm doing some good yet real frustrating that we don't seem to be getting anywhere with the crime in this area. I guess, given the budget the county allows us, it isn't surprising. Over all, I'd say I'm nowhere near ready to quit."

"That's good to hear. It is a fact, we do need you on the job. You and Dale both. In my opinion, he's far and away the best sheriff we've ever had in this county. At least, in my memory."

"I'm glad you think so because he is. Now, do you have any suggestions as to who I should talk to about that club?"

"For now, I'd prefer you don't talk to any of the kids unless it's absolutely necessary. Be best if they're all told about it at the same time. It'll be somewhat easier for them and at least help to hold down the rumors that always go along with this sort of thing."

It was with a fair amount of frustration that Mack left the school. The only satisfaction he felt was the knowledge that Harley Anderson was already working on his list of things he wanted done with his new fortune. A fortune that he was sure now he could do some good with.

With the schools, the computers were only a start and far less important to Mack than the new laboratory equipment he knew Harley would be ordering as soon as possible. Mack especially wanted to see the Biology Department better equipped, and with a special emphasis on the environmental sciences. It was only through education, Mack knew, that people's attitudes toward the environment could be improved. It might be a futile effort, but he had to try to do what he could, especially with money he had no use for himself.

CHAPTER 5

MACK RETURNED TO THE MOTEL after leaving the school. By then, the medical examiner for Clayborne County was there, along with a forensic expert from the Minneapolis police department.

"I figured you'd get someone to help, Dale," Mack said after briefing him about what little he'd learned at the school, "I didn't think you'd be able to get anyone this quick though."

"Neither did I," Dale said. "Your friend Paul Danielson got involved. He talked the Minneapolis Police Department into helping us. That speeded things up considerably."

"How did you get Paul involved?"

"I just mentioned his name when I was talking to them about getting some help. They called him, called me right back, and said the forensic guy was on his way. He got here quick because he was just finishing up with a murder on the north end of the cities."

"Well, I'm real glad we got someone. I've got the feeling that this is going to be a difficult murder, no matter how much help we get."

"Me too. So when are you meeting with Paul?"

"Why do you think I've already set up a meeting with him?"

"Simple. The only way he and his department would have responded the way they did is if he already knew about what we're up against. So when is it?"

"Tomorrow morning, at Katie's, with you and me. He's taking a few days off right now, so I didn't see any sense in waiting on this. We do need his help, Dale."

"I know. It bothers me that you're paying for it. I know that even if you don't care about the money, this still isn't right. Especially since we both know the county could afford it, if the idiots running it wanted to."

"Yeah, well, let's worry about that later. Right now, all I want to do is get this murder solved before anyone else is killed."

"I know, Mack. Somewhere down the line this crap the rich around here are pulling has got to stop, and I think you and I ought to do our best to see that it ends."

"I agree, Dale. And some time we will at least slow down their crap. Especially when we nail Mr. Eric Von Herter."

"That would be one hell of a good start, wouldn't it?"

"It would. And since there's not much I can do around here right now, I think I'll head for home."

"You might as well," Dale agreed. "You've put in a long day as it is, even without counting your run-in with the poachers."

The first thing Mack did when he got home was take his dog, Charge, a huge Newfoundland, out of his kennel. Normally, Mack took his dog with him every day. He didn't this time because he had hoped to return home before he started his normal day.

Charge was initially happy to see Mack, and he wagged his tail so vigorously his whole body undulated with his excitement. Until he remembered that he'd been neglected all day. Then he turned his back on Mack, stuck his nose in the air, and walked away. Knowing he had to soothe the animal's hurt feelings, Mack found his favorite retrieving dummy and walked out on the dock on Heritage Lake. The ice was thick and the snow fairly deep, but Charge wasn't able to restrain his delight in being able to play the game with Mack. He was soon out plowing through the heavy snow drifts covering this part of the lake, chasing the dummy. Neither the cold nor the snow did anything other than increase his joy. To Charge, deep snow and cold weather only added to what he considered a great game. With his heavy coat, snow and cold were never a bother.

Mack's father, Ben, soon joined them on the dock. His curiosity about Mack's day was none too subtle, especially after he saw the grim look on Mack's face, when Mack would normally be smiling, if not laughing, at his dog's antics.

"You want to tell me what the hell's wrong now, Mack?" Ben asked. "The meeting with Harley go that bad?"

"No, the meeting with Harley went fine. We've got another murder, Dad. And this one looks bad."

"That's not good. Not good at all. You and Dale have any idea who did it?"

"None."

Charge returned to the dock with his dummy, dropped it by Mack, and greeted Ben the way he normally greeted people he knew and cared about. First, he pushed his nose between Ben's legs and lifted his head vigorously, then jumped up and dropped his massive paws on Ben's shoulders, licking his face, leaving liberal amounts of slobber there.

"This damn dog is nuts," Ben complained, failing to hide his grin.

When he finished with Ben, Charge decided that Mack was okay after all and gave him the same treatment.

"I think your dog gets a little too friendly," Ben grumbled, still trying to hide his smile.

"A bit, yes," Mack agreed, trying to smile without managing to find one.

"So did your day have any good in it?" Ben asked, still curious about Mack's meeting with Harley Anderson, while not wanting to push it too hard. He knew that Mack was very troubled by the murder he was dealing with.

"Sure, Dad, my day did have some good in it. I caught a couple of Von Herter's cronies out in the refuge this morning, poaching deer. I made a citizen's arrest, then for the hell of it, I used my shotgun on the fuel tanks of their snowmobiles. It blew the hell out of them. They claimed the machines belonged to Von Herter, so I did get a great deal of satisfaction out of it."

"I imagine you did, Mack, but what's it going to cost? You know Von Herter isn't going to let you get away with that without raising some royal hell about it."

"Von Herter isn't going to do a damn thing about it. According to Harley, he's got some cash flow problems right now, so he isn't going to be able to pull his usual crap. He can't afford to fight me on this one. It just flat will cost him more than he can spend."

"Now how the hell are you going to manage to fight a legal battle with him? You damn sure don't make enough to hire a lawyer for ten minutes, let alone to beat a man like Von Herter, whether or not he's got cash flow problems."

"You're right, I don't make enough on the job to fight Von Herter. If he goes after me or the department, this time, I will beat him at his own game. Even Von Herter has limits as to how much he's willing to spend to collect the money two snowmobiles are worth. Not to mention that if he goes after anyone for the money, his ass is going to land in jail for poaching."

"There's something in the way you said all that, that's got me wondering. What did go on with your meeting with Harley this morning? I got a feeling now, there was something serious to it."

"There was. Mandy had a will. I inherited most of her money."

"How much was there? I don't see her being rich enough to leave you the kind of money it would take to fight Von Herter in court. Not if he really wanted to go after you anyway."

"No, she wasn't, but..." Mack told Ben about the money and where it came from.

Ben smiled as Mack talked, then chuckled when he finished. "Leave it to Jason to outsmart himself that way. If he's dead, I'll bet he's rolling over in his grave right now, knowing you're the one who got his money."

"He would. And that's part of the reason I accepted it. That and the fact I know I can do some good with it."

"I'm damn glad you had the sense to see that. Now you can help out Bob Anderson and his family. Lots of others too. You know, Mack, having money isn't all bad, if you know what to do with it."

"No, I guess not. It is a hell of a burden though. A lot more of one than I ever wanted."

"I doubt, Mack, that it's much worse than those you're already carrying around on your back, given you tend to carry everyone's burdens there."

"I guess you're right. I learned about some other things today. Important things you and I and I think Roy and Wanda need to talk about. Fairly soon too."

"Now you've got me real curious, Mack."

"I hope so, Dad. I really hope so."

Mack left Ben then, loaded Charge into the back of his pickup, and made a visit to a young man who, through an act of courage, saved Mack's life, then because of some quick thinking, saved Mack's dog Charge's life.

Johnny Earle had paid a high price for what he did for Mack, by losing his job, and then having his new pickup destroyed by some men who didn't like it when Johnny helped Mack.

So now Mack intended to pay him back as much as he could with his newfound money, even though he knew that there really was no way to pay him back all the way.

"What can I do for you, Mack?" Johnny asked when he answered Mack's knock on his door.

"Nothing much," Mack explained. "I just want you to take a little ride with me."

"Why? Did I do something I shouldn't?"

Mack had to laugh at that question. "No, Johnny, this isn't about anything like that. I just need you to come with me for a bit."

"Well, okay."

The pickup Johnny had once owned was a Ford F150, so Mack took him to the Ford dealer.

"My dad is thinking about buying a new pickup and asked me to check them out for him. You seem to know the good ones, so I thought I'd bring you along to see what they have, and which one you think is the best and has the best accessories."

"Hell, I don't think you need me for that, Mack. You probably know more about it than I do."

"No, I don't, and I'd really like to have you check out the trucks."

A salesman found them then, and the three of them moved through the lot. Johnny was the one who checked out the trucks, while Mack watched to see how Johnny reacted to each one. When he got into a deep red one with a quad cab and nearly every accessory possible, his eyes lit up.

"I don't know for sure what your dad wants in his truck, Mack," he said, "but this truck has it all. And I love the color. Man, what I wouldn't give for a truck like this."

Mack smiled. He knew this was the right truck for Johnny. "Did you ever think, Johnny, that maybe you already gave more than enough to earn this truck?"

"Naw, I never did any damn thing that could earn me a truck like this."

"Actually you did. I'm not going to tell you what it is you did to earn it because it'll be good for you to puzzle over it for a while, as to how you did earn it. The thing is, this truck is yours. All the insurance and any other costs, including taxes, connected with it, will be taken care of."

"You're joking with me, aren't you, Mack?"

"I would never do that to you. Any more than I'll ever forget who and what you are. So go with this gentleman here, and he'll take you into their office so you can sign all the papers connected to the truck. I'm going to take off now, but don't worry about a ride home, you'll be driving your new truck."

Johnny was too shocked to even answer Mack, who left him standing there shaking his head.

Mack felt good about what he'd just done, and the fact that he was going to do it again, even though it would take a fair amount of time before he got to everyone on his list.

CHAPTER 6

H E RODE FAST AND ALONE across the lake. He had no desire to see or be anywhere near other snowmobiles or those who might be riding them, so he broke his own trail. He loved the feeling of his machine every time he flew over a hard wind-packed drift and the way it sent clouds of snow flying when it landed at the bottom where it was softer. Even though the full moon was a few days past, the night was bright and clear, so he needed no lights.

He had no destination in mind. He just wanted to run free, far away from the cares of his world. A world he wanted to forever leave, if only he could. Since that was impossible, he took all the joy he could from the short time he was allowed to be out and alone with the wind in his face and only the sound of his machine and the solitude of the wild country around him.

When he reached the far side of the lake, he took to the woods, not minding the slower pace. Here, his solitude was even greater.

Avoiding anything that had even the slightest appearance of a human-made trail, he made his own or followed the few made by animals who, like him, avoided the humans who so often brought only death and destruction to most of the wild places they touched.

He wasn't familiar with the area he rode through and didn't know or understand this or any other wild place, so he was soon lost. At first he didn't care, then gradually panic began to overtake him, and he drove erratically and too fast through the woods.

When he was sure he would never find his way out, he suddenly found himself at the edge of a large clearing. A clearing made by huge machines. Machines built to rip out trees and tear up the earth to level it for more new buildings which were going to be part of Heritage Preservation Minnesota, the new resort being built on the now shrinking Clayborne National Wildlife Refuge.

He was safe now, he knew. There would be construction roads to lead him back to the county road that brought him there. So he drove slowly through the clearing, curious about the machines and the massive destruction they had been built for. As he reached the far edge of the clearing, he noticed a small building sitting alone, far away from the other construction equipment, and decided to see what it was for.

It was so clearly marked he knew what it was well before he reached it. Smiling, he stopped his machine and walked up to the building marked Explosives. There was only a small padlock securing the door, and he knew it wouldn't take much to force it open.

He didn't have anything with him to get it open but knew it wouldn't be any problem to bring something along next time he came back. And he would be back. All he had to do was pay close attention as he drove out of there and he would be able to find this place again.

And next time, he would have the tool he needed with him to take what he wanted from the shed. Once he had it, he would have the power he had been longing for. With it, he could do things he couldn't otherwise do. Not even with a gun.

It was with a light heart and a big smile that he drove home to the place he didn't want to be.

CHAPTER 7

MACK LIVED ANOTHER RESTLESS NIGHT, filled with the kind of dreams that frequently plagued him since the death of his wife. This time, the dreams were of cold water and someone dying. Dreams, he was sure, caused by the murder of a woman he'd known for only a short time, who died in dark cold water. Kristin was a woman he knew he would never forget.

So Mack was out of bed early and on his way to Kingsburg equally early, for his morning meeting at Katie's Kafe with Sheriff Dale Magee and Minneapolis Detective Paul Danielson. This day, however, he did remember to bring along his dog, Charge, who was now sleeping contentedly on a small mattress in the covered back of his pickup, even though the early morning air carried a brittle cold.

Riding in the warm cab of the truck, Mack almost felt guilty about the dog riding in back, all the time knowing Charge would have it no other way. The cab of the pickup was too confining and too warm for him. As long as he could curl up on a reasonably soft place out of the wind, his heavy coat kept him as warm as he wanted to be. The only problem he ever had with weather was heat. Cold never bothered him. In fact, when it was as cold as this day, it was when he seemed to be most in his element.

So Mack spent little time worrying about the dog. Instead he tried to focus on the meeting he was about to have and the day ahead. He also wasn't looking forward to the short meeting the banker

Harley Anderson requested. Mack knew it was necessary. He simply wished it wasn't. There was too much to do that he considered more important. Like solving the murder of the construction worker, Gary Baldwin.

Mack was sure that this time, the murder was his responsibility to solve. And it could prove to be too much for him.

He was the first to get to Katie's and was on his second cup of coffee when Dale joined him, thirty minutes before the time they'd scheduled for the meeting.

"You're here awful early, Mack," Dale said as he sat down. "You have trouble sleeping or something?"

"Some. I had the cold-water dream again. I haven't been bothered by it or others much lately, so I was hoping they were coming to an end."

"Was this dream the same as the others you had when Lisa Anderson was kidnapped?"

"Almost. Only this time, I heard a lot of people screaming. That part was new."

"You know, Mack, I do wish you'd stop having those dreams. It wasn't too long ago I wouldn't have paid any attention to them, other than worry some about you not getting enough sleep. Now I know better. It seems now like you're dreaming more about something that hasn't happened yet than you do about the past. It scares me sometimes."

"Me too, except this time I think they were about Kristin. No matter how much I wish it didn't, the way she died still haunts me."

"I guess it would. Only try to shake it off. What happened to her was in no way your fault."

"Yeah, well even if my brain tells me you're right, there's something else inside me that says otherwise."

"Try anyway, Mack."

"I will. So what did the forensic guy and the medical examiner have to say?"

"The medical examiner said the cause of death was obvious. He'll tell us more about what the man was up to after the autopsy. The forensic guy dusted for prints and will run what he found through the computer. He found some fibers from various types of clothing, which he'll examine in the lab and let us know about. The most interesting thing he found was a few strands of red hair. Hair he thought came from a female. He'll let us know that for sure later too."

"Damn" was all Mack could say.

"Okay, Mack, what is it? I know you've got something stuck in your craw all of the sudden."

"Yeah, I do, Dale. The red hair. I sure hope Teresa Lorring is still in Iowa."

"So do I, although I hadn't thought about her until you mentioned her. And if she isn't, you won't be the only one having bad dreams. I'm just as responsible as you are for her never being prosecuted after what she was doing with those boys."

"I didn't think at the time, and I still don't think, that what she did was near as bad as the law might say it is. The thing is, she was pretty screwed up while she was having sex with them, so if she hasn't been getting any help, there's no telling what kind of mess she might be now. From what I know about her, I don't think she's capable of murder, but I don't know how the hell you ever know for sure."

"You don't Mack, and that's the problem. There's not really any way to ever know for sure. Do you want me to check on her for you? Kathy hasn't said anything about her coming back, but she might know about it if she did. Teresa is, after all, her aunt."

"It's my job so I'll be checking into it today, the first chance I get. I'll talk to Linda Sanders first. Even if Kathy is Teresa's niece, Linda is Teresa's sister, so she is the one who'd most likely to know whether Teresa's here or not."

"That's a good start. I'll ask Kathy about her tonight too. She talks to her folks fairly regular. If none of them know for sure though…"

"I'll make some calls to Iowa. One way or the other, I'll find out what we need to know."

Before they could discuss Teresa Lorring any further, Paul Danielson arrived. Mack introduced him to Dale as soon as he sat down.

"I have to tell you, Mack," Paul said to start the conversation, "your asking me here to talk about doing some consulting work came as one big surprise. Especially since you've told me in the past about your sheriff's department having serious budget problems. What happened to change them?"

"Nothing the county's done, that's for sure," Dale said.

"The thing is," Mack interrupted before Dale could tell Paul where the money was coming from, "the department does have the money now, so it's no problem. Our problem now is getting a handle on the amount of crime we have around here. Especially the most recent murder. We really need help from someone like you, Paul, and that's what this is about."

Dale shook his head as he listened to Mack, then said, "Mack, there's no way we're going to ask Paul to help unless you're honest with him. I know you don't want anyone to know what you're doing, but you can only carry that just so far. He has a right to know."

"What are you doing, Mack?" Paul asked. "Working with no salary at all now? I damn sure don't want to be the cause of something like that."

Dale explained, "If you take on this consulting work for us, he'll be paying for it."

"How the hell are you going to manage that, Mack?"

"It's a long story, Paul," Mack said. "But Dale's right, you should know what this is about."

Paul sat quietly until Mack finished telling him about Mandy's will, only occasionally shaking his head in disbelief.

"I don't think," he said then, "I've ever met anyone quite like you, Mack. If it were me with the money, I'd be picking out a big RV and planning my first trout fishing trip. Something similar anyway. Why the hell aren't you?"

"I guess I don't have a real good answer for that question, except I don't need a big RV to go fishing. And maybe it's because there are a lot of people around here I really care about."

"It's a lot more than just people, Paul," Dale said while staring into Mack's eyes. "He cares as much about the way this earth of ours is being raped as he does people. And he cares even more about the Clayborne National Wildlife Refuge. What's left of it anyway."

"I think," Mack said, "that's enough discussion about me and what motivates me. The question is, Paul, are you interested in doing some consulting work for us?"

"Very much. I'm going to have to think on it for a while before I can make a decision. It wouldn't hurt to talk it over with my wife either. If she ever talks to me again, that is."

"That sounds fair to me," Dale said.

"It is fair," Mack also agreed. "But would you mind giving us the rest of the day today. You did say you're taking a few days off, didn't you?"

"I did. And yes, I'll give you today. And I mean give too. I don't want any money for it. Not yet. Part of the reason I'm willing to do it is because I'm real curious about the way your last murder was committed. We can talk more about that later. I am going to have to talk to my wife about all of this first. If I decide to take the consulting work on a regular basis, it would be a definite asset if she'd go along with it. Not to mention, I've been thinking about retiring. Having something like this to do part of the time will make it much easier."

The three of them finished the meeting discussing the murder of Gary Baldwin, the dead man found in the motel.

The comment Paul made that interested Mack the most is when Paul said he'd only seen a similar stabbing once.

As they left Katie's, Dale asked Mack, "So what's up for today?"

"First," Mack answered, "a short meeting at the bank with Harley. Then I'm going to check on Teresa Lorring. After that, I'm going over to the high school. If nothing else, I want to talk to Lisa Anderson. She's one kid who knows me well enough to talk to me and to give me some honest answers, if she has any answers to give me. Whether she knows anything about that DR club or not remains to be seen."

"That sounds like a good start, Mack. Give me a call sometime this afternoon, so we can coordinate what we've learned. I should have more information from both the medical examiner and the forensic guy by then."

"Will do."

As soon as he left Dale and Paul, Mack went to the bank. The lobby had just opened, so Mack was somewhat surprised at the number of customers already inside. He was even more surprised to see that two of those customers were Teresa Lorring and Linda Sanders.

He stopped for a moment, watching the two women. Teresa was a few years younger than Linda, although it wasn't at all obvious. Both were beautiful, and Linda still looked far younger than her actual age. Even her blond hair was still natural, with only a few small streaks of gray. Teresa's face, however, was beginning to show the many hard times she'd had.

Teresa was arguing with the bank teller when Mack finally approached the two women.

"I still don't see why you can't cash my check," Teresa argued. "Even if it is from out of state. I banked here for years, and Linda banks here now."

Overhearing the argument, Mack approached the women.

"Good morning, Linda, Teresa," he said. "How are you two this frigid Minnesota morning?"

"Well, hello, Mack Thomas," Teresa said with a big smile. "What a treat it is to see you so soon after getting here. How are you?"

"Good…real good. I couldn't help hearing you when I came in. Is there a problem?"

"Yes," Teresa said, her voice somewhat agitated. "This person," she pointed at the teller, "won't cash my check. She says it's bank policy to not cash personal checks from out of the state."

Mack smiled at the teller. "Cash the lady's check please. If you have any questions, call Harley Anderson and tell him that Mack Thomas requested that the bank make an exception to its rule in this case."

The teller glared at Mack for a moment, made the call, then immediately cashed Teresa's check.

"Thanks, Mack," Teresa said as they stepped away from the teller's window. "It seems as though you're always doing me some kind of favor when I see you."

"It's no big deal. So what brings you up here from Iowa? Have you been here long?"

"No, I just got here a few days ago. I'm thinking about moving back. Both of my folks are gone now, so Linda is the only close family I have left. And family is extremely important to me now. After all that's happened, it sometimes seems as though family is all that matters."

"There sure isn't much, if anything, that matters more," Mack agreed. "So how have you been otherwise, Teresa? I hope life is treating you better than before you moved back to Iowa."

"I think you mean, don't you, Mack," Teresa said with unusual frankness, yet with a smile, "have I gotten any help with my problem. The answer is yes. A lot of help in fact. Both one on one with a very good psychologist, and lots of time spent in-group with other sex offenders, men and women. And let me tell you, the time in-group spent with men was decidedly unpleasant. Unlike almost all the women, they, for the most part, seem to think what they did was okay. It wasn't. It wasn't okay for any of us to do what we did. And for my part, I can promise you, I'll never do it again. When I think of my behavior now, it makes me rather sick." As she watched the shock from her words wash over Mack's face, her smile broadened. "So tell me, Mack, how is that dear father of yours? I certainly hope everything is okay with Ben."

"Yes, he's fine. But I have a meeting with Harley Anderson that I'm already late for. Are you going to be in town long?"

"Why?"

"No special reason. Other than I thought we might have a cup of coffee together after I finish. If you're going to be around and if the two of you have time."

"I would really love to have a cup of coffee with you, Mack," Linda Sanders said, speaking for the first time, "and I know Theresa would too. But we both have appointments today." She smiled, and Mack could tell from the look in her eyes that she meant it when she said she'd love to. "Hopefully, next time you want to have coffee with me, I will be able to."

"I'll look forward to doing it another time."

"Me too, Mack," Teresa said, "Just call me when you get a chance. I'm staying with Dave and Linda."

"I'll do that. Now, I've got to go."

Mack went into his meeting with Harley Anderson with his mind far more filled with Linda Sanders and Teresa Lorring than it was with the details about the money he and Harley were going to discuss.

CHAPTER 8

Lisa Anderson, Terry Holstrom, and Jo Stuart became instant best friends at the beginning of the school year. They originally got to know each other because of an environmental organization called STR (for Save the Refuge). Lisa was the one who came up with the idea to start the group, which was primarily for high school students.

Terry and Jo were the only two people that came to Lisa's first meeting. There were over fifty members now, but that first meeting started a friendship which grew steadily for the nearly three months since they first got together.

Lisa and Jo had casually known each other during several years of going to the same school without ever being real friends. Terry was new to the school that fall. Terry and Lisa had a common bond that cemented their relationship the instant they met in the school hallway on the first day of school.

Both girls were kidnapped the previous summer by the same two men and used as prostitutes by the men. They'd only met once during their ordeal, when Terry risked a beating to bring Lisa a glass of water. Lisa managed to escape fairly soon after she was taken, so as brutal as it was for her, Terry's horror was even more brutal and lasted far longer. Lisa had something else happen in her family, which to her was far worse than her own experience. Her mother was shot in the head by the same men who kidnapped her and was just beginning to make a recovery.

They'd only talked about their experiences to each other once, yet it gave them their bond and an understanding of each other uncommon for two girls so young.

Although Jo hadn't shared their experience, her cousin, Cheryl Holstrom, went through a similar experience at the same time and was now in the state mental hospital with little hope of recovery.

So the three girls shared experiences that separated them from their classmates and went beyond their young lives or anything they should have ever experienced.

They also shared a love for the environment and a concern about the steady degradation of it. Especially the environment where they all lived, Clayborne County. Even though Lisa was the one who had gotten the idea for STR, they all had worked equally hard at bringing it to the point where they could actually accomplish something.

The principal of Kingsburg High School had given the girls permission to use their study hall time to meet in the cafeteria. That's where they were this morning, sharing a bowl of fruit that Terry brought along.

"I don't really like grapes much," Terry said when she brought the fruit, "but I thought you guys might."

"I love 'em," Jo answered, taking a bunch.

Without commenting, Lisa picked out an apple to eat while they talked about an event they were in the early stages of planning.

"I suppose," Jo said, "we should have it on a weekend. Like maybe a Saturday afternoon?"

"That's probably the only time we'll get enough people," Lisa agreed.

"Wouldn't it be better to do it on some special time?" Terry asked. "Like maybe Thanksgiving. If people would come out that day and we could get enough of them on that bridge to actually stop the traffic for a while, I think it would mean more."

"I don't think," Lisa said, "that we can get it organized by then. It's a good idea though."

"I think so too," Jo agreed. "It's too bad we can't do it on Christmas. That would really mean something."

"It sure would," Lisa agreed, "only I don't think we could talk many people into a protest march on Christmas. Even if we do find enough people who care about what they're doing to the refuge."

"Let's do it New Year's Eve," Terry suggest. "What better time to try to make some changes than at the end of one year and the beginning of a new one."

"You know," Lisa agreed, "you're absolutely right. People are always making resolutions and stuff then."

"I agree," Jo said, "I think New Year's Eve would be the perfect time to hold our rally. We might be able to get a lot of people to come then."

"And best of all," Lisa said as she watched Terry pick up a banana and slowly peel it, "we have plenty of time to get it organized."

Lisa continued to watch with fascination as Terry finished peeling her banana and pushed it deep into her mouth. She sucked on it a moment, slowly pulled it out of her mouth until just the end was still there, then savagely bit it off.

All the time she was working on the banana, Terry's stare was empty, more as if she was looking inside, rather than at any of her surroundings. After she bit the end off it, she looked at Lisa and smiled.

Before Lisa could comment to Terry about what she was doing, Mack Thomas joined the girls. As soon as he did, Lisa totally forgot about Terry and her fruit-eating antics. Mack almost always had a strong effect on Lisa when he was around. She was sure she was in love with him, and marrying him some day was the biggest goal she had in her young life.

For Mack, her ideas about him simply made him uncomfortable. He currently had another woman in his life who, like Lisa, was in love with him. Beth Cheman was currently living with Lisa Anderson's family, to assist Lisa's father Bob with all the work involved in raising a family and running a dairy farm. Beth had been there since Lisa's mother, Margaret Anderson, was shot.

Mack's mind was far away from all that as he sat down with the girls. He was focused on the murder of Gary Baldwin and it showed on his face.

"Is something wrong, Mack?" Lisa immediately asked.

"I'm afraid so," Mack said, his voice grim. "There's been another murder. One of the construction workers at the new resort. Do any of you know anything about the group around the school called the DRs?" Mack first looked at Terry, then the other two girls.

"We all do, Mack," Lisa answered. "From what I've heard, it's some kind of snowmobile club. I think the DR stands for Drag Runners. Something like that anyway."

"That's what it is," Jo said. "They go out mostly at night. My cousin, Skip, went out with them once. He said it wasn't much fun. He hasn't gone since that first time."

"Where do they run at night? Do any of you know?"

"I'm not sure, Mack," Lisa said. "I think that at least part of the time they go over in the refuge."

"Skip never told me where they went the night he was out with them," Jo said, "so I don't know for sure where they go."

"I don't know for sure either," Terry said, "but I've heard they go into the refuge a lot."

"Is there anything else you can tell me about them? Like who belongs to the club?"

"I know some of them," Lisa said, then gave Mack their names.

When Lisa finished, Terry and Jo gave Mack a few more names. And some of the people Terry named were adult males.

Jo explained to Mack that her cousin Skip lived with her family, then gave Mack Skip's full name and the classes he would be in that day.

Because of a student meeting going on in the auditorium during the next hour, Mack decided to wait a while before talking to anyone else at the school. He left it, and not quite sure what to do next, he called Dale with the cell phone he hated, to see if Dale had learned anything from the medical examiner or the crime scene investigator.

"I haven't seen the autopsy report yet, Mack," Dale told him. "I did talk to the medical examiner. He had a couple of interesting things to tell me. Whether or not they'll do us any good, I don't know—"

"That's something we'll have to wait and see," Mack interrupted. "So what did he tell you that was so interesting?"

"You know, Mack, I was getting to that."

"I know. Sorry. I guess I'm over-anxious about this case."

"I understand, Mack. Anyway, the examiner found a couple of half-chewed grapes in the guy's mouth. He hadn't had intercourse. We'll know more when we get the full report."

"It's pointing more and more toward a redheaded female, isn't it, Dale?"

"It is."

"And Teresa Lorring is here now. She's staying with her sister Linda. I ran into them at the bank this morning."

"Damn, I was hoping we could rule her out right away. Now I guess we'll have to talk to her."

"Let's wait on that for a while, Dale. I don't know for sure why, I've just got a feeling in my gut, after talking to her, that she didn't do it. I know it's only a feeling, but it's a damn strong one. And she isn't the only redhead in Clayborne County. Hell, I just finished talking to one."

"Yeah, and I know one pretty good too. I'm sure Kathy didn't do it though. Especially since she was with me at the time of the murder. How about the one you just talked to? Is she a suspect?"

"Not hardly, Dale. She's just a kid. A friend of Lisa Anderson. They were having one of their STR meetings when I stopped by the school. They gave me the names of some of the people in that DR club. Two of them that Terry mentioned were adults. I thought I'd wait until the school is finished with something they had scheduled in the auditorium before I talk to anyone else."

"Good idea, Mack. It isn't likely any of them will be much help anyway."

"It's hard to say, but you're probably right."

CHAPTER 9

MACK SPENT A FRUSTRATING AFTERNOON, talking to some of the members of the DR club. The only thing any of them would say about the murder victim was that he was a nice guy. As far as where they rode their snowmobiles, they all swore they never went anywhere near the refuge.

Mack knew they were lying. They didn't even try very hard to hide the fact they were lying. Mostly, they acted as if they were above the rules that applied to everyone else. Skip Halbertson, Jo Stuart's cousin, didn't have an attitude problem, but all he would tell Mack is that he went out with them once and it wasn't much fun. He also said that he didn't know what the DR initials meant.

When Mack talked to the school principal, Dan Locks, about the boys, he told Mack, "Their attitude isn't so surprising when you consider the families those boys come from. If their parents aren't rich, they certainly are well to do. As far as we know, all of the boys in the club are athletes, so for most of the kids in this school, they are the elite, the heroes. It's no wonder, with the definite class system we have in this country, that they think they are above the rest of us."

Mack knew Dan was right. The truth in what he said didn't make it any easier for Mack to swallow. So when he got home that evening, his feelings were written on his face.

"Bad day, Mack?" Ben asked him when they sat down for supper.

"It was mostly just frustrating." Mack went on to tell Ben about his day.

"Well, there's nothing new in their attitudes," Ben said. "It just sounds to me like things pretty much never change. There's nothing like money and status to send people down the wrong path."

"True. So I guess you and I, Dad, had better watch ourselves, or we'll be as bad as they are. Now that we're both rich."

"I don't think I'll have to worry about you, Mack."

"I hope not. All that money is too big a burden."

"Maybe, but I hope you hold on to enough to cover emergencies, should you ever have any. Which, given the way you approach life and your job, it's highly likely you will."

"Given the way I was raised by you and Roy, I don't know any other way to do it, with either my life or my job. And speaking of Roy, did you talk to him yet?"

"I did. He damn sure didn't want to come now, no matter what the hell you've got on your mind. You know how much he hates winter here."

"I know. Is he going to come? What we need to talk about is important."

"He is. Not why you want him to though. He's doing it for Wanda. She's had a couple of bad dreams. That cold water thing again. Have you been having them?"

"Just one."

"The same as before?"

"Close. They're somewhat different this time. This time, people are screaming."

"The same as Wanda's then. I sure wish you two would stop with those dreams. They're scaring the hell out of me and Roy."

"If I could, I would, Dad. What's important, though, is that Roy and Wanda are coming."

"They are. I don't suppose you want to tell what it's about now do you?"

"I could. I rather not because it's going to take a fair amount of time to do it, and with all of us together, it'll be easier to make the decisions that need to be made."

"Okay, I'll wait until they get here. It won't be that long, given how Roy pushes things sometimes. And you know, Mack, it's not that I mind at all that you've been helping out a lot of people. I just don't want you helping so much you hurt yourself."

"I know. I will be careful with the rest of the money from now on. Just don't expect me to keep too much for myself."

Ben laughed. "There's no way I'd ever expect you would."

"Good. Now I have a question to ask that I wish I could avoid, but sooner or later, because of what has happened and is happening, I have to ask."

"So ask away, Mack. There's nothing you haven't been able to ask me in the past, so there shouldn't be a problem now."

"It's about Teresa Rolling."

Ben's face colored. "Nothing ever happened between us, so why do you have a question now? We only went out that one time."

"You're an excellent judge of character, Dad, and you did know her a little better than I did." Mack went on to tell Ben about the evidence found where Gary Baldwin was murdered, and Teresa being back in the area when it happened. He finished with "So do you think she's capable of murder?"

"Not hardly, Mack. I know she did some things with those boys that wasn't right. Not the way she did them anyway. But murder? I definitely do not believe she's capable of it. If she were, she would have done it a long time ago, starting with that no-good husband of hers. And he had it coming. Knowing what I know now about that murdering, thieving sheriff, I wouldn't blame her now if she did kill him. He's thankfully dead and gone by his own hand. Did us, the county, and everyone in it a real big favor, too, when he did himself in. At least now, we have a real sheriff. I doubt we'll ever find a better one than Dale. Having you as his deputy has proven a good thing too, even if I'd far prefer that you were doing something else.

"No, Mack, I think too much time has gone by since he died and all the rest happened for Teresa to come back here now, just to murder some guy. And if she were to do something like that, why would she do it here where she'd be suspected? That would be way too stupid for an intelligent woman like her to do. She's made some real bad mistakes, used some real poor judgment. Murder? No way. All I can say is, if you spend much time on her while you're looking for the person who killed that guy, then you're going to be wasting time looking at the wrong person while the real murderer is still out there. Look somewhere else."

Mack sat for a moment, staring at his father. He couldn't remember when, if ever, that Ben had said so much at once, let alone without even taking a deep breath. So he was fairly sure that he would not spend a lot of time looking at Teresa Rolling as the murderer of Gary Baldwin. He couldn't completely rule her out, but he had far too much respect for his father to not heed his words. He knew, too, that Sheriff Dale Magee would agree with him. There were few, if any, people Dale respected more than he did Ben Thomas.

"Well, Mack," Ben finally said when Mack's silence continued, "what do you think."

Mack sighed. "I think you're right." He smiled. "I surely do hope to hell you are anyway. I like Teresa, and I hope, and have hoped all along, that she has gotten herself together. I really want her to have a good life. She deserves better than what she's had so far."

"I'm glad you feel that way. I think she's had enough hurt, without being a suspect in something like this. And if you see her again, in town or whatever, tell her I said hello."

"Why don't you tell her, Dad? She's staying with Dave and Linda Sanders. We do have their phone number."

"I don't think so. She might get the wrong idea if I was to do that."

"What wrong idea? There's nothing wrong with being friendly."

"Being friendly is one thing, giving someone the idea you might be interested in something else…well, I don't believe I want to do that."

"Do you really believe that a simple friendly hello to Teresa will give her the wrong impression?"

"I do. For now, I do."

CHAPTER 10

A LIGHT SNOW WAS FALLING WHEN Mack left the house, making the dark Minnesota night even darker. The large flakes were dancing a slow waltz in the quiet air as he drove the county roads to the Anderson farm. The snow wasn't needed, given there was already over two feet on the ground. Even so, it gave the night a peaceful feeling it otherwise wouldn't have.

Mack wasn't all that fond of winter and hadn't been since his years following rodeo primarily in the southwest, where winters were never near as harsh as Minnesota's typically were. Nights like this one though, when he was alone traveling over empty country roads, he couldn't help loving the serenity.

The lights were still on in the dairy barn when he drove into the farmyard. Mack didn't go inside because he knew that it disturbed the cows when anyone went in there at milking time, even if he was a frequent enough visitor for them to know him. Instead, after letting Charge out of the back of his pickup, he walked around the barn to a small addition where the horses were kept in the winter months.

As always, Lisa's big gelding, Lancer, immediately greeted him, nuzzling Mack until he gave the horse his sugar cube treat. The rest of the horses followed, with the exception of Mack's horse, Dare, who steadfastly ignored him.

"You being a snob again, Dare," Mack asked him, "or just a twit?" He laughed when Dare continued to ignore him. The animal's attitude was almost a ritual.

Then Charge came ripping around the back of the barn, crawled through the corral fence, and started a game of tag with Dare. They went at it for several minutes before Dare relented and walked over to Mack, obviously expecting a treat. Mack gave him one.

The barn door opened, and two women came out. Lisa Anderson was first. She was followed by Beth Cheman, who had been living with the Andersons to help out since Lisa's mother was shot the previous summer.

Both women were in love with Mack, and Mack loved them back, only in very different ways. Beth was his lover, and Lisa was only a friend. She wasn't yet seventeen and wouldn't be for another month, so she could not be anything else. Not in Mack Thomas's world.

Lisa knew that Mack and Beth cared very deeply about each other. However, not wanting to hurt her in any way, they both consistently avoided any kind of physical contact in Lisa's presence. Even so, Beth couldn't hide the smile she had for him. Lisa didn't try to hide hers.

"I'm kind of surprised to see you tonight, Mack," Beth said. "You usually call me first."

"Yeah, Mack," Lisa added, "you do."

"I know. I mostly came over to just to say hello and to see Dare before he forgets who I am. It's been a while."

"It has," Lisa agreed, then with her characteristic bluntness asked, "did you catch whoever murdered that guy yet?"

"No, we haven't," he answered, purposely not mentioning that they were sure the killer was a woman. He knew that the less he said to anyone about the case at this stage, the better. The only exception to that rule, outside of law enforcement, was his father. His uncle Roy would be too, when he got to Minnesota. Both men could be totally trusted with anything they were told and had assisted Mack in the past with difficult cases.

"There's other weird stuff going around here besides murder, Mack," Lisa said. "I don't suppose you know anything about it, do you?"

"Yes," Beth added, a scowl on her face. "Do you know what some of those things that are going on are about?"

"I've been too busy," Mack answered, "trying to solve a murder to know about anything going on. What's so weird that's going on?"

"Didn't you notice," Beth asked, "the two new cars in the driveway?"

"No."

"You should have. Three guys from the Ford dealership in Kingsburg came here today. Two of the cars they were driving were for Lisa and me. They were paid for and already registered in our names, with the insurance on them paid for. A full year's coverage. It's strange enough, Mack, that we would suddenly have someone give us new cars. What makes it stranger is the fact that the car for me was exactly like one you and I looked at a couple of months ago, when I was wishing I could afford a car. So what do you know about it?"

"Nothing. You know I don't have any money."

"Another thing, Mack Thomas," Lisa said. "My dad wants to talk to you. Weird stuff has happened to him too. He was balancing his checkbook today, and when he called the bank to double check on his balance, there was a lot of extra money there. I think he said it was something like fifty thousand dollars. This is all too weird, Mack."

"It does sound strange," Mack agreed. "I wish I could help, and I would if I could."

"Somehow, Mack," Beth said, "I think there's parts missing in what you're saying."

"Now, Beth, do you really think I would leave out anything if I had any answers for you."

"I do," Lisa told him.

"I don't suppose," Beth asked, "you have time to go out for a beer, do you? Chores are done, and it won't take me long to clean up. I shower fast. And it would be nice to have a long conversation with you tonight."

"Only if it's not too long. I've got a tough day ahead tomorrow"

"Good. I'll only be a few minutes."

"I know you don't want to talk about it, Mack," Lisa said as soon as Beth left for the house, "but do you have any idea who the murderer is? It's about all anyone at school talked about today. Except Terry. She doesn't ever want to talk about things like that."

"After what she's been through, it isn't surprising she wouldn't."

"I know, but I went through it too. Not everything she did..."

"I know, and for that, I am really sorry. It should never have happened."

"Stop it, Mack. Stop it right now! I know you blame yourself, but it damn sure wasn't your fault. So just stop it! Please."

"Okay, Lisa, I'll do my best."

"You always do your best. That's why I love you so much. Now wait here for Dad. He'll be out in a few minutes."

With that, she quickly turned and left him standing there. She went back inside the barn without looking back. She just didn't move fast enough to hide her tears from him.

By the time Beth joined him again, he was completely miserable, wishing that there were a way to live without ever hurting anyone. Especially the way Lisa was hurting. Yet he knew that there was almost nothing he could do about it. The only solution to the problem was for her to find someone her own age and stop focusing on him.

Bob Anderson came out of the barn a few minutes later.

"I have only one question, Mack. Did your dad do all this for us?"

"And I have only one answer to that, Bob. Absolutely not. You have my word that my father had nothing to do with it."

"I'll take your word on that, Mack. I just somehow suspect you know more than you're saying. And I surely do wish I knew where the help is coming from. It's all way too much. Money in the bank, bills being paid, new cars, and most of all, someone's paying for both a physical therapist and speech therapist for Margaret. That damn sure isn't being done by the insurance company. Those bastards don't even want to cover her hospital bills."

"I wish I could answer your questions, Bob. I just can't."

"Okay, Mack, I understand. You two have a good time tonight."

Beth silently took his hand as they walked to his truck. Charge joined them and gently nudged Mack's other hand, letting him know that he too understood Mack's pain. He then went back where the horses were stabled, to wait as he always did when Mack and Beth went out, on his own small pile of straw kept in a corner for him. He was far happier there than he would have ever been inside the house, where he would have been more than welcome.

The short ride to the bar in the very small town of Glentago was made in silence. Beth knew from experience that Mack wouldn't want to talk until they were inside.

They sat down at the farthest from the bar, corner table there. The waitress knew them and brought them a pitcher of the brand of beer they always drank while they were there. Beth ordered a variety basket of appetizers to snack on while they talked.

"I hope," Beth said, "you're going to tell me what you really know about what's going on, Mack."

"I don't think I have anything to tell you, Beth."

"What you mean is that you don't want to. I know you well enough now to know when you're not telling me everything. No matter what the subject. I know you do it sometimes because you don't want to hurt me. This time, it's different, and I really don't understand why you don't trust me enough to tell me."

"That's not it at all, Beth. I do trust you."

"Now I know you know at least some of what's going on. If you didn't, you wouldn't have answered me the way you did."

"Sometimes, you're too smart for my own good. And I do have reasons for not wanting to talk about all this."

"Why not? What did you do, rob a bank somewhere so you could help people?"

Mack laughed. "I never thought anyone would look at it that way."

"I don't really think you would," Beth said, a big smile spreading across her face. "This conversation, however, has gone far enough to tell me that you are somehow for sure involved in everything. So why don't you admit it and tell me what it's all about."

"It has never been that I don't trust you, so much as I think it's better that not too many people know what's going on. It makes it easier for me if they don't."

"I don't really understand that. So would you please tell me? I give you my solemn word that I will never repeat any of it."

"You're making this real difficult, Beth," Mack told her, frowning slightly.

"I'm for sure not trying to make anything difficult for you, Mack. I just want to understand."

"Okay, I'll tell you since you've promised not to repeat it. And before I start, I want you to know, I'll hold you to the promise."

"I wouldn't expect anything else from you."

"Okay, but hang in there with me. It's a long story. It starts with your cousin, Jason…" Mack went on to tell her all that happened that led to his inheriting the money and why he didn't want anyone to know what he was doing with it.

"That's an incredible story, Mack. Do you really think, though, that you really have to keep it such a secret?"

"It's more that I'd really like to. Also, like I already mentioned, someone as proud as Bob Anderson is going to be very unlikely to accept the help he needs right now. Not to mention how deserving he is. And that's why I don't want Lisa to know what all this is about right now. I don't think she'd be able to keep it a secret from her dad."

"I think you deserve at least some credit for what you're doing."

"No, Beth, I definitely do not deserve any credit for anything. I never earned a dime of that money, and if I thought it would have ever been put to some kind of good use, I never would have accepted it. I didn't want it and I don't need it. It's mine now, only because I think I can do some good with it."

"Couldn't you do more good if people knew you wanted to do some decent things?"

"Not hardly. If people in general knew what I'm doing, I'd be driven nuts by everyone and his brother with their hands out. It will work better this way. Also, I will be working with some people, that

I've given my word to keep their identity secret for now, who believe we can turn around some of the harm that's been done around here."

"I don't suppose you're going to tell me anything about that, are you?"

"I promise I will tell you about it soon. Just not now."

"Okay, Mack. I understand and I do appreciate that you've told me as much as you have. I don't suppose I can convince you to take me somewhere that we can be alone for a while, can I?"

"Not tonight. Very soon though, and I'll have a surprise for you then."

CHAPTER 11

MACK ARRIVED AT KATIE'S KAFÉ a half hour before his normal morning meeting with Dale. He was surprised to find Paul Danielson already seated at the table where he and Dale always met.

"I didn't expect you this early," Mack said as he sat down, "but I'm really glad to see you, Paul. You've got good news for me, I hope."

"I'm not so sure you having to put up with me as much as you're going to is good news or not, Mack. I have decided to take you up on your offer to do consultant work for your department. More than that though, I've decided to retire from full-time police work."

"Your wife didn't object to you retiring?"

"No one could be more surprised about how this is turning out than I am. She not only did not at all object, she's extremely excited about it. Money's not going to be a problem since I've got more than enough years in to draw my pension. That really helped us decide what to do next. She wants to move up in this area, so she can quit her job and start growing vegetables for a living."

"She doesn't mind leaving all her friends behind?"

"She informed me that she never liked her job. As far as friends go, we've never been what you'd call sociable. The real friends we have will always be friends. A few miles won't change that." Paul paused a moment as his face filled with a broad smile. "She wants us to buy some land. If it already has a house on it we can live in, fine.

If not, she wants to build one. She wants to farm, organically, if you can believe that?"

"Has she always been interested in farming, Paul?"

"So she says. She always gardened. I just never paid enough attention to it to know how interested she was."

"Are you going to buy some land then?"

"I don't see any way around it, Mack. If she's willing to let me start over this way, it's only fair I let her do the same thing. The biggest thing is how to get started. I don't know a damn thing about any of it."

"You'll learn, Paul. And it won't be near as difficult to get started here as it would be somewhere else. Dale's on his way in the door now, so I don't have time to tell you why today. When we have time, I'll explain it all to you."

"You're getting mysterious again, Mack."

"Not really. I'm just a little short on time today."

"I'm glad to see you here already, Paul," Dale said as he joined them at the table. "Are you bringing us good news?"

"If my accepting your offer is good news, then I brought it."

"It is. When can you start?"

"Today. I'll need a day this week to finish up in Minneapolis, clean out my desk and all that. Otherwise, I'll be totally available."

"That's great. I'll let the county know what we're doing today."

"Remember to keep me out of it, Dale."

"I will, as much as I can."

"I know, just don't tell them about the rest of it."

Dale smiled. "I can't tell them what I don't know, Mack."

"Good. Do you think they'll try to give you any problems about all this?"

"They'll probably try. I don't think they can do anything though, as long as I stay within the budget. If they try anyway, I'm sure a leak or two to the radio station and newspaper will force them to back off. It'll be more than a little embarrassing if the public finds out what's going on. Especially the way they handle the county budget."

"It might be a good thing, then, if they do object. It might help to turn things around in this county."

"It might. Did you learn anything new yesterday?"

"Not much. The boys in that DR club are mostly a bunch of smartass liars. They all claim they aren't running their snowmobiles in the refuge. They don't try very hard to hide the fact they're lying though."

"That all?"

"Pretty much, other than I talked to Dad last night about Theresa Lorring. It's his opinion that we'll be wasting a lot of time and effort if we make her our number one suspect. He doesn't believe there is any way that she could be capable of murder."

"Before you two get any deeper into your discussion on your new murder case, I'd appreciate it if you could fill me in on all of it. If I know what's going on, I might be able to help. That is what you hired me to do, isn't it?"

"Sorry about that, Paul," Mack said. "It's just that we're not used to having the kind of help you can give. Before we get into it though, I have to warn both of you that I'm going to have to keep my end of it short. If Dale will give me a few hours off this morning, I have a few things I need to do today."

Dale laughed. "Given your high pay rate, Mack, I don't know if I can afford to give you any time off."

"I'll take that as an okay," Mack said. "Let's meet at the Hanging Kettle about one, after the worst of the noon rush is over. Show Paul what a real cheeseburger is. You two should have Paul's contract ready by then and maybe have time to show him around town some. I can take him out in the county this afternoon. Then he can ride with me until he knows his way around a little better."

"Sounds good," Dale agreed.

Mack gave Paul a quick rundown of what he knew and was doing in connection with the murder of Gary Baldwin, then left them. He drove to a local real estate office to meet one of the agents. He didn't know which agent he would be meeting with because Harley Anderson set up the appointment for him. It was a pleasant surprise when the agent turned out to be Linda Sanders.

"I didn't know, Linda," Mack said as they got into his truck, "that you were in real estate. Having you as my agent today is a nice surprise though."

"I'm glad you think so. I'm your agent today because I asked to be. I thought it would be nice to spend some time with you, even if I don't sell you anything."

"I kind of feel the same way. Spending time with you is a nice thought, even if I don't buy anything. So how long have you been in real estate?"

"I was only doing it part time for the last five years. About six months ago, I decided I'd had enough of computer programming and the long commute to the cities. So I quit my job and went full time. It turned out to be a good move, the way real estate has been selling."

"I'm glad to know you're doing well, but I have to say, I'd like it better if things were the way they were before that damn resort was built."

"I can understand that real well, Mack. Dave's been bitching about it a lot, even though his construction business has doubled since all this started."

"So what can you tell me about the land we're going to look at today?"

"It's four hundred and twenty acres, with about three hundred open. The people who own it raised beef cattle, so a lot of it has been in pasture. About fifty acres are wooded, and the rest is low ground. Most people would call it a swamp. I'm sure you'd call it a wetland. The Saint Catherine River runs along the far side of the wetland area. It runs higher than it did before the damn was built. Not high enough to have much effect on anything else though."

"What about the buildings? Are they in decent shape?"

"The house is older but in great shape. It's a large three-bedroom rambler with an absolutely beautiful kitchen, two baths, and a full finished basement. There's also a small guesthouse. It's only one bedroom, one bath with no basement. It's also in very good condition. The barn and outbuildings look to be in decent shape too."

"It sounds good. And the price seems to be more than fair enough, everything considered."

"Speaking of the price, Mack, I am curious about one thing. How can you afford it on a deputy's salary?"

"It's not for me, Linda. I'm looking at it for my Uncle Roy. He and his wife, Wanda, are hoping to move back to Minnesota, and they're looking for a place to raise cattle. Roy's been a rancher in Texas for a long time."

"Why would they want to move back here, cold as it is?"

"It's a family thing. It's true that they aren't very fond of the weather. They'd like to live closer to Dad and me anyway." Mack had trouble keeping a neutral look on his face as he talked, given that most of what he said wasn't true. Roy and Wanda had no idea that he was doing what he was doing.

"When will your uncle be able to look at the property?"

"In the next couple days. He and Wanda are on their way to Minnesota already."

"Well, I sure do hope you and they like the place. The people who own it have been good neighbors, and Dave and I have been a bit worried about who or what might end up owning it. I showed the property to Eric Von Herter about a month ago. He made an offer on it that was so low, it was insulting. I was very happy that he wasn't willing to pay anywhere near the full price. God only knows what he'd do to the place."

"He'd destroy it somehow, I'm sure," Mack said, hoping now that this would be the right place, so he could buy it out from under Von Herter. "Do you and Dave live close to this property I'm going to look at, Linda?"

"Next door. Dave and I bought our farm about six months after we left San Francisco and moved back to Minnesota. We love it there, and like you, we don't want to see too many changes."

Mack knew as soon as he turned into the driveway that he'd found the farm he wanted. After touring the house, the guesthouse, and the outbuildings, there was no doubt in his mind. When he was taken out on a tractor, through the deep snow and near the river, he was excited about buying it.

By the time he joined Linda back in the house, he was ready to make his offer. Linda could tell by the look on his face when he walked in, that he was ready.

"Do you want to go out to your truck to talk about it, Mack?" she asked.

Mack smiled. "Do we have to?"

"It would be a good idea."

"There's no need for that," said Emmett Schulte, the man who owned the property. "Emma and I will go downstairs so you can have some privacy. It's too cold to be sitting out in your truck."

"I take it you like the place, Mack," Linda said as soon as they were alone. "Can you make an offer, or do you have to talk to your uncle first?"

"I can make an offer now. My offer is the asking price, and since they want to sell the furniture and the appliances in here and the guesthouse, I'm willing to buy them, and I'll buy all the machinery they want to sell too. Can you write it up now?"

"Yes, as soon as they agree to your offer."

"Okay. Talk to them. I want to get this done right now. I really love this place. And having you and Dave for neighbors is a plus."

"Thanks for the compliment. Having you for a neighbor will be a plus for us too. And I can see that you do love this place, Mack. The thing that has me wondering is, if this is for your uncle, why are you so excited about it, and are you sure you can make this kind of a commitment on your own?"

"I'm excited because I will be a part of this when Roy and Wanda take it over. Yes, I can make a commitment like this. Tell Emmett and Emma to come back upstairs. And, Linda, as soon as this is settled, I'll be writing a check for the full amount. I'd like to get it done in an hour or so. I really do have to get back to work."

"Come on now, Mack. You are kidding, aren't you?"

"No, Linda. I'm very much not kidding. I really do have to get back to work."

"Mack, you know damn well that wasn't what I was talking about."

Mack laughed. "I know. Now, if there's any question about my writing a check that size, call Harley Anderson at the bank. Tell who ever answers the phone that you are calling about the business I'm dealing with today, and they'll let you talk to him. Any other questions?"

"Oh, I think I have a bunch. I also think that what I really want to know is none of my damn business. I do have one legitimate question though. When do you want to take possession?"

"Yesterday, but Emmett and Emma can have as much time as they need to move."

"Okay, Mack. And I don't have to call Harley. I can't imagine you writing a bad check for any amount, not to mention one this size."

"Good, that means it'll all go quicker."

It took more than an hour, but when Mack and Linda left the farm, Mack was the proud owner of four hundred and twenty acres. He also had the keys to the guesthouse, so he could keep his promise to Beth.

Linda was happy too. She had just earned her biggest commission since she started selling real estate.

"I'm running a bit late," Mack told Linda Sanders as they left the farm. "So how would you like to have lunch with three cops?"

"Mack, after the commission I just made today, all because of you, I'd love to have lunch with you anywhere and with anyone. I don't have any appointments this afternoon either. So where are we going?"

"The Hanging Kettle. Martha makes the best cheeseburgers money can buy."

"Sounds good. Dave and I eat there occasionally, when I feel brave about my weight. Who are the other two cops?"

"Dale and the new detective who just started doing consultant work for us today."

"How did the sheriff's department manage to hire a detective? Even just as a consultant. All I ever hear from Dale is that the budget is so small, you weren't even getting full pay. What changed?"

"I don't really know for sure. Dale's been constantly fighting for more money. I guess he's finally gotten some."

"Mack, I really like and respect you. You've done a lot of good things since you've been a deputy sheriff. But you are a lousy liar. I'm not going to ask you any personal questions, and I don't expect you to tell me anything about what's going on. I just want you to know I know all of the good things going on around here have something to do with you. What you did today, and the way you did it, proved it to me."

"Right now is not a good time to tell you anything, Linda. Someday though, I promise I will."

"Fair enough, Mack. It's been great doing business with you." She laughed, then leaned over and kissed him on the cheek. "If I were younger, I think I'd enjoy giving you a lot more than that."

"You wouldn't have to be any younger, Linda. You're a beautiful woman. The fact that you're married to a great guy, however, would make it impossible for both of us."

But Mack did his best to hide the fact that part of him wished she could give him more. He now had a strong feeling that there was something between them, a feeling not like any other he'd ever had. One that was never going to go away.

"The part about the great guy *might* be true," she said, obviously having the same feelings as Mack, "but then, it might not." She stopped talking and gently kissed him on the lips.

He responded to it, and they were surprised at what happened, but both obviously savored the moment. Mack looked into her wondering eyes, then quickly started driving. Her hand was on his knee and stayed there.

Mack and Linda were just sitting down inside the Hanging Kettle when Dale and Paul arrived. Martha Fuller, the lady who owned and operated the café, came to the table even before Dale and Paul had the chance to sit down.

"Bacon cheeseburgers all around," she said, making a statement more than asking a question.

"Sure," Mack agreed, "unless Linda wants something else."

"What the hell," Linda said, smiling, "after the money I made today, I guess I can afford to put on a few pounds."

"If you were with Mack Thomas today," Martha said, "nothing that happened to you would be a surprise. So what brings this odd group together? Two cops, a real estate agent, and a total stranger. What could be going on that I don't know about?"

"Nothing much, Martha," Dale told her. "Our friend here has just come to do some work for the sheriff's department. Meet Detective Paul Danielson. Paul, this is Martha, the owner of this place. And this lady with Mack is Linda Sanders, the mother of my fiancée."

"Pleased to meet you, Detective Paul Danielson," Martha said. "I'll go put the burgers and fries on. Later, if you people can see fit to do it, I'd sure like to know what this little meeting is about."

"What is with her?" Paul asked. "She sure is nosey."

"Yes, she is," Mack agreed. "And she knows more about everything that's happening in Clayborne County than you can imagine, so we always have to be careful what we say around her. We come here because she makes the best cheeseburger money can buy."

"Speaking of money, Mack," Dale said, "Linda must have been the one you had the appointment with today?"

"Yes," Linda said, looking at Mack and momentarily resting her hand on his leg a fair amount above his knee. "I was. I took Mack out to look at Emmett and Emma's farm. Which he bought for his Uncle Roy or so he says."

"That was a quick decision," Dale said. "Did you put down a big deposit on the place then?"

Linda laughed. "No, Dale, he didn't. He bought the place. Wrote a check for the full amount. He owns it now."

"Jesus, Mack, how the hell could you afford to spend that much?"

"It wasn't a problem. I was just acting as Roy's agent. He wanted me to find him a place before he moves back to Minnesota."

"Why would Roy do that? He hates winter."

"A lot of reasons. Most of them family." Mack smiled, then turned to Paul. "So what do you think of Clayborne County so far?"

"I think I'm going to like it here. I know you have many of the same problems as we have in the cities, but not near to the scale they have there."

"No, they aren't. At the same time, we don't have near as much to work with as they do. Hopefully, that will improve somewhat in the future. If the county can ever get its priorities straight."

"That's a lot to ask for, Mack," Dale said. "Right now, they're about to raise hell about my hiring Paul to do the consulting work. There's not a damn thing they can do about it and they know it. But they're going to try to raise hell anyway."

"Let them try," Mack said, very much feeling the effects of Linda's hand on his leg, but he managed to keep talking anyway. "They push too hard, and they are the ones who will look bad, not you." Without paying attention to what he was doing, he dropped his hand down on Linda's knee, then quickly pulled away as he realized what he was doing. She smiled.

"I know, Mack. And in some ways I hope they push this too far. It's time some new commissioners were elected. Maybe we'll eventually get a few with brains."

"Don't they have complete control over your budget, Dale?" Linda asked, finally letting go of Mack's leg.

"Of course they do."

"Then how can you spend money for a consulting detective if they tell you that you can't?"

"As long as I don't go overbudget, they do not have control over who I hire. And I'm not going overbudget."

"Where's the money coming from then?"

"Some of it is coming from the salary Mack used to be getting and isn't any longer. The rest is strictly confidential. If I could tell you more, Linda, I would."

"There are a lot of things going on I wish someone could tell me." Linda smiled and looked at Mack. "If I could read his mind," she said to Dale as she nodded toward Mack, "I think I'd find at least some of the answers."

"I think we'd all like to read his mind," Paul said, as Martha delivered the food to their table.

"Whose mind?" she asked as she set the baskets of fries and burgers in front of them.

"Eric Von Herter's," Mack said to throw Martha off track.

"All you would find there," Martha told him, "is a whole lot of evil."

"You are right about that, Martha," Dale agreed. "He is one very bad person."

"I take it he's one of the bad guys around here," Paul said, then bit into his bacon cheeseburger. "Oh my god, this is awesome."

"They don't get any better, Paul."

Martha was about to join them near the end of their meal when Dale's cell phone rang.

"Damn it," he said as he answered, "I told them not to call me for anything less than an emergency." His face was ashen when he hung up. "We've got to roll," he said, "there's been another murder."

"Where, Dale?" Mack asked. "I'll meet you there as soon as I drop Linda off."

"It's at Eric Von Herter's estate."

"I know you're in a hurry," Linda said when she was ready to get out of his truck, "but there's something I want to give you."

With that, she moved her hand behind his head and kissed him. And kissed him with far more passion than either of them would have expected. It surprised him, but he matched her passion with his own. The kiss was not a short one.

"That," she said, "meant more than you think, Mack Thomas." Then she quickly left the truck.

Mack thought about Linda all the way to Von Herter's. Every time he'd ever been around her, there'd been some kind of attraction between them. It left him wondering, but somehow feeling better inside than he had in a long time.

When Mack got to Von Herter's estate, Paul Danielson was standing outside one of three small houses located behind Von Herter's mansion. Von Herter was there, obviously upset with Paul.

"You will do exactly what I tell you to do!" Von Herter screamed, as Mack walked up to them. "I own this county, and I can have your badge in a minute."

Mack stepped between them. "Listen, you fat asshole, if I ever see you harassing anyone who carries or wears a badge in this county again, I'm going to arrest you for assaulting a police officer."

"You can't call me an asshole, Thomas, and you can't threaten me, or I'll have your goddamn badge too."

Mack jammed a finger hard into Von Herter's chest. "You've tried threatening me before. Don't ever do it again. Have you forgotten what happened last time you tried? It wasn't me who shit his pants."

"You ain't got your uncle here now, boy."

Mack jammed him again. "No, I don't. Do you really think I need them to deal with a fat pig like you?"

"Yeah, I do." Von Herter moved like he was going to take a swing at Mack.

"Go ahead," Mack told him, smiling. "Throw a punch at me. Then, after I finish beating the living hell out of you, which I certainly will do, I will arrest you and I will make sure you stay locked up this time. And if I don't, I will have Roy find you when you're alone. Would you like that, you scumbag little prick?"

"You can't threaten me."

"I just did. Do something about it."

"Well, you just can't…"

"Get the hell out of here before I beat the hell out you just for the fun of. It would definitely make this a good day. Even better than buying the Schulte's farm was."

"Better than what?"

"You heard me. Now get the hell out of here before I actually get pissed."

Van Herter just stood there staring at Mack, his face filled with hate. Mack grabbed his shoulder, turned him around, and pushed him. "Now move on, or I am going to arrest you."

Von Herter slowly walked away.

"Jesus, Mack," Paul said when Von Herter was far enough away, "that was not something I would have expected to see you do. You really hate that man, don't you?"

"Hate, Paul, is mild way of putting the way I feel about him. What was he bugging you about?"

"Mostly, he tried to tell me how we were going to handle the investigation into this murder. When I told him I didn't need his advice, he got a bit irate."

"What can I say, Paul? Of all the people in this county that need to be locked up, he's on the top of the list. So there is no way I will ever put up with him or anything he says or does."

"I know how you feel. I've met a few like him."

"So what's going here? Who was killed?"

"The guy who did the maintenance around here. His name was Jim Patterson. He was gut shot with a shotgun. It's a real mess. The medical examiner is in there now. As soon as Dale's available, the three of us have to have a serious conversation about this and the other murder. There's something about them that has me real curious."

"That's why I wanted Dale to hire you, Paul. Most of the time, I feel inadequate when this kind of thing happens. It's one thing to raise hell with the drug dealers the way we've been doing since Dale became sheriff. That part of law enforcement we seem to be handling. This kind of thing, though, and I'm out of my league."

"That's your opinion, Mack, not mine. Now, while we're waiting for Dale, tell me about your uncle Roy I keep hearing about. The one you supposedly bought a big farm for."

"I did—"

"Don't give me that crap. You can lie to that nice real estate lady all you want. Not me or Dale. Now tell me about Roy."

"There's not much to tell. He helped raise me when my mother died. He's a great guy, but he's not someone to be messed with. He's never taken any shit from anyone and I don't think he ever will. He's smart, owns a small cattle ranch in Texas, and has made most of his money trading."

"Trading what?"

"Just about anything. He buys things, sells things, and trades things. And he always seems to make a few dollars with every deal. He's also helped solve some of the crimes I've worked on since I became a deputy. It was Roy and my dad who found Lisa Anderson after she escaped from that home for girls."

"And now he's planning on moving back here, after living in Texas for how long?"

"A lot of years. The truth is though, he isn't planning on moving here. I'm just hoping I can convince him to do it. And it isn't only because I'd like to have him here, it has even more to do with some of the things around here I hope can be changed for the better."

"Which are?"

"It has to do with the environment, the refuge, and that damn resort. Some of what we are trying to do will make it easier for your wife to start farming. But I'll have to explain it later. Here comes Dale."

Dale was shaking his head when he joined them. "What a mess."

"What did the medical examiner have to say?" Paul asked.

"That there's no question as to what killed him. Getting shot in the stomach twice with a twelve gauge at close range did the job. The forensic team is going over everything now, although there's damn little hope of them finding much. The only thing I can see so far that's connected to the other murder is the guy's jacket. It has a big DR on it."

"Well," Paul said, "aside from the DR thing, there are two things that I find real curious."

"What are they?"

"The way the two guys were murdered."

"They were completely different," Dale argued. "One was stabbed in his open mouth, the other shot with a shotgun in the stomach. How could that be related?"

"Well, as Mack might remember, both of us have seen two murders very similar to these."

"I'm not sure I follow you, Paul," Mack said.

"Think back to last summer and the murders in that home for girls. How were two of those men killed?"

"With a shotgun."

"That's right. The fat one was gut shot. This guy here had one hell of stomach on him too. And the third guy was stabbed with a

82

sharpened butter knife. It took someone a long time to sharpen that knife."

"Damn," Mack said. "I never would have made that connection. Do you think this has to do with drugs too, Paul?"

"Mack, you know as well as I do that those killings had nothing to do with drugs. I didn't want to do anything to the people that did them, so I blamed the murders on a drug war. I'm still not much interested in who did it. And I hope to God I don't have to be. It's just that there were connections to what happened there and some of the people that live in this county. It might all be way too much of a coincidence. If we get a third murder, with some guy's face blown all to hell, we'll know there's a connection."

"It's possible, I guess. What do you think, Dale?"

"To tell you the truth, it's something I don't want to think about, even if I do have to."

"One thing to remember now though," Paul said, "it could very well be just a coincidence. I only brought it up so that we do considerate it a possibility."

"Another possibility is Von Herter. We know that he's behind or at least involved in most of the drug traffic in this part of Minnesota. He was a good buddy of Genysis Paul, who owned that home for girls, not to mention the judge that frequently used the girls there. The day Von Herter came to lay some serious threats on me at my dad's, the two goons he had with him were Nate Bear and that Lennie character. They were two of the men murdered at that home."

"You're right, Mack," Paul agreed. "There are plenty enough connections there, to keep a close eye on him. The thing that has me wondering, though, is the fact that the first guy, that Gary Baldwin, was killed by a woman."

"Von Herter hasn't got the guts to do any killing himself. He could have hired someone to do both of the murders. Both of them could have been done by the same woman or he could have hired two different people."

"The question there is, why. What's his motive?"

"I guess, Paul, that's the reason Dale hired us. To figure it out."

Paul laughed. "Mack, I was hired. You were appointed. It was a good appointment on Dale's part, but that's what it was."

"Either way, we have to figure it out."

"That, Mack, is a for damn sure thing."

By the time Mack, Paul, and Dale finished up at the murder scene, the late afternoon sun was casting dark shadows over the cold Minnesota landscape. Paul rode with Mack as they left for Kingsburg.

"How about telling me now, Mack, a little about some of the things you, and I have no idea who else, are planning to do around here?"

"To start with, we want to help people who are serious about farming organically to get started. In a lot of cases, we will be able to help with financing, which is usually difficult to get. We also hope to set up some kind of training facility, to make some of the things people need to know about farming organically easier."

"You're not talking about some kind of communes, are you?"

"Anything but. Everyone involved will be independent as far as their own farms are concerned."

"People farm on their own all over. Other than financing and training anyone can get from an agricultural college, what's going to be different?"

"Colleges mostly teach people how to use chemicals. Organic gardening and farming is done without chemicals. Marketing the products produced is always difficult. Often, that can be done better on a coop basis. We want to set up—" Just then Mack's cell phone rang. It was Ben.

"I hate to be bothering you, Mack," he said. "Roy and Wanda are here now. The thing is, they're hungry, and I was curious as to when you plan on getting here?"

"I was heading to Kingsburg. Is the food ready now?"

"It will be shortly.'

"Do you have enough to set an extra plate?"

"When don't I?"

"Okay, Dad. If I'm not there in a half hour, eat without me. Otherwise, we'll be having company."

"Good enough. Just know that we'll be having pot roast, beef and pork both, cooked together in the big roaster, baked squash to go along with the potatoes and carrots, and fresh out of the oven apple pie for dessert."

"Okay, Dad, I'll keep that in mind."

"What was that all about?" Paul asked.

"My dad wanted to know how quick I'd be home. My uncle Roy and his wife have arrived and supper is about ready. Since your wife is still down in the cities, how'd you like to join us for a damn good home-cooked meal?"

"I don't know, Mack. I wouldn't want to intrude on a family get-together."

"You would be no intrusion at all. Besides, you're curious about Roy, and this will give you a chance to meet him. You might as well do it now anyway. There's no way you'll be working for the Clayborne County Sheriff's Office and not meet all of them."

"If you're sure…"

"I'm sure. And it'll give you a chance to learn more about the ideas we have about farming and all the rest of what we were talking about."

Wanda ran out to greet Mack as he got out of the truck. She wrapped her arms around him, pulled him close, and kissed him. "Damn, but it's good to see you, Mack."

"It's good to see you too, Wanda," he said, then turned to Paul, staring at them in disbelief. "This is Wanda, Paul, Roy's wife. Wanda, this is Paul Danielson, the new detective consultant in the sheriff's department."

By then, Roy and Ben had joined them, and Mack made introductions all around.

"Nice to meet you, Paul," Roy said, "now let's get the hell inside. I ain't used to this damn Minnesota cold."

"Okay, Mack," Roy said as soon as they sat down at the table to eat Ben's great cooking, "tell me what all of this is about. Coming here for a winter visit isn't what I'd call something I wanted to do."

"Which part do you want me to start with, Roy?"

"The dreams you and Wanda are having would be a good place. The two of you are enough to make a man crazy."

"I can't really explain them." Mack looked at Wanda. "What are yours like?" he asked her.

"A lot like those other cold water dreams we had last summer, Mack. Except this time, there's ice and people screaming. And somewhere in the background, something about swimming. I always wake up before I know why."

"Mack," Paul said, "you mentioned something about dreams when all those things went on last summer. Did Wanda have them then too?"

"Those two seem to do this kind of thing now and then. Some kind of psychic connection, I think," Roy said. "And when they have it, it's never a sign of good things to come."

"The thing is," Ben said, "Mack's had some bad dreams for a long time. Mostly they were about the past. Now it seems, since they both have them, it's always something that's going to happen. What we're all hoping is that this time they're about past things."

"That's right," Roy said. "So what do you think it is, Mack?"

"I really don't know. Wanda, what do you think?"

"I don't know for sure. I only know that it scares the hell out of me. As far as it being about the past, why are they different?"

"I wish to God I knew."

"It doesn't look," Roy said, "like we're going to solve the problem right now. Maybe with us being here, the two of you will get over them, although I doubt it. So we'll have to wait and see. Now, tell us about the rest of it, Mack, if you can?" Roy looked at Paul, then at Mack, the look on his face asking Mack if Paul could be trusted.

"To start with, Roy, I want to tell you a little about Paul. He's the detective that helped me out during last summer's troubles. He's working for Dale now because I wanted him here. We need someone with experience, and he's an experienced homicide detective. He also started just in time, given there was another murder today."

"Who was it?"

"The maintenance guy at the Von Herter estate."

"Well, at least this time, you've got some help. So can you tell me what else is going on?"

"I can't tell you everything tonight. There's too much to tell, so I'll give you a quick rundown. I'm sure Dad told you that I inherited some money. It was a fair amount. Since then, I've been working with Kalif Anderson, Harley's son, on some ideas to try to improve at least some things around here. One of the things we most want to do is turn this area into a place where farming is done the way it ought to be done, rather than the way it's most often done. Not just raising vegetables the way Dad does, but including dairy, chickens and eggs, hogs, beef, and any other crops or animals. The beef part is where you come in, if you're willing to get involved, Roy?"

"Just how do you think I can do that? Wanda and I live in Texas, so as much as I'd like to help you with this project, I don't really see how I can."

"You could if you moved back to Minnesota."

"There isn't much I wouldn't do for you, Mack, you know that. But move back here, now that's a hell of a lot to ask. You know how bad I hate winter. Not to mention, I doubt I could afford to start any kind of a beef operation here with the way things cost now. I'd need near three hundred acres to do anything."

"What if I was to tell you that I know a place to start that you can afford?"

"I doubt that."

"Don't doubt it, Roy," Paul said, a big smile on his face. "He does know all about the right place for you."

"And how do you know that?" Roy asked Paul.

"I spent an interesting lunch with Mack today. I met some interesting people too. One lady in particular. I think I'll let Mack tell you the rest of it though."

"Okay, Mack, tell me all about it."

"Sure. If you had four hundred and twenty acres with a house, barn, pole building big enough for some of the cattle in the winter, all the equipment you need to put up hay and whatever else you might need, would that be enough to start?"

"Of course, it would. Only I doubt I could afford it. Even though I've got a nice ranch it Texas, it's not going to bring me enough to pay for what you're talking about."

"What if I told you that you don't have to sell your ranch? You've already got help down there, and we can get you help here. I'd be part of that help. In fact, I'd be your partner here."

"Who the hell's going to come up with that kind of money?"

"Me. The truth is, Roy, today I bought the place I've been telling you about. If you're willing to go partners with me, all you have to invest in the operation is your time and expertise. All I ask is that we raise grass-fed beef and never use any hormones, drugs, or any of the other crap that's being done on almost all beef operations today."

"I don't know how much money you have, Mack, and I don't care. I can't let you do something like that for me."

"Why not, Roy? If it were the other way around, you'd do it for me. You'd do it for Dad too, for that matter. After all the things you've done for me in my life, if I can't do something like this for you, then what's the point in doing anything for anyone?"

"This setup you're talking about, does it mean I can spend part of the winter in Texas?"

"It does."

"Be damned. Wanda, what do you think of this crazy man's ideas?"

"Roy, I think it sounds totally wonderful. Absolutely the only bad thing would be if we had to spend all winter every winter here. We won't have to, so let's do it. Please, Roy, I really would like this."

"I guess I would too," Roy said. "Having more time with Ben and Mack would be a good thing, not to mention you having more time with your family. Just one thing. This ain't going to bust you, is it, Mack?"

Mack laughed. "Not even close."

Roy stood and reached across the table, taking Mack's hand. "I guess we've got a deal."

"You sure don't screw around when you get an idea," Paul said, "do you, Mack?"

"I guess not. There is one other thing though, while we're on the subject. When I was looking at the farm I bought today, I asked Linda if she had any good listings of smaller places for sale. So you and I will be taking a little time, between murders, to look at some of them."

"I'm going to have to get my house in Minneapolis sold before I can buy something."

"I know, Paul. It doesn't hurt to look though. And if your wife is really serious about organic farming, she should think about going to work for Dad in the greenhouse. There isn't as much work now as there will be when he starts the plants for spring planting, but I still think he can keep her busy part time. He's been an organic farmer for a lot of years, and I'm sure he can teach her a lot to make getting started easier."

"She might want to get a job at first," Paul said.

"Makes no matter," Ben told him. "Even this time of the year, I could hire her on full time. The greenhouse needs tending seven days a week. It'd help a lot to have another adult around full time during the week."

"It seems as though you've got everyone's life planned, Mack," Paul said. "Why are you so anxious to do so much for everyone else?"

"I'm doing it for me more than anyone. There are a lot of things happening I don't like and that bothers me, so I'm trying to change some of them."

"Not to mention," Wanda said, "Mack is one of the kindest, most generous, most decent human beings you are ever likely to meet."

"She couldn't be more right about that," Roy added.

"He also tends to try to carry the weight of every kind of problem there is on his own shoulders," Ben said, as he always did when anyone talked about Mack.

Paul looked at Mack. "This is one hell of a family you've got. I'm glad you talked me into coming here tonight. It has been a real pleasure meeting them."

"That's enough of that now," Roy said, trying to make his voice sound gruff, but failing miserably. "When the hell are Wanda and I going to get to see that new farm of ours?"

"Tomorrow. It's easy to find, and I'll call Emmett and Emma in the morning to let them know you're stopping by."

"Sounds great, Mack. It sounds just great."

"Oh, and one other thing. I've got the extra key to the guest-house. I'll be using the place now and then, if you and Wanda don't mind?"

"I don't hardly think either one of us would ever be doing any complaining about it."

"Roy couldn't be more right about that, Mack," Wanda said.

CHAPTER 12

IT WAS STILL REASONABLY EARLY when Mack dropped Paul off in Kingsburg, so he decided to go to the Anderson farm to pick up Beth and take her to the new farm. He knew she would be pleased when he showed her the guesthouse. She was just finishing up the supper dishes when he got there.

"What's up with you tonight, Mack?" she asked when she opened the back door of the old farmhouse for him.

"Not too much. I have something I want to show you tonight, if you have time to go out for a while?"

"That was a dumb question," she laughed. "Of course, I have time. I always have time for you and you know it."

"Good, as soon as you're ready, we'll go. Where is everyone else? I should say hello before we leave."

"James," she said, referring to Bob Anderson's father, "is already in bed. Bob, Lisa, and the kids all went to town to do some grocery shopping. I'll leave a note for them. Do you mind if I take a quick shower? I still smell like the barn."

"I don't mind at all. It would be nice if you smelled good tonight."

"Why, Mack Thomas, what is it that you have in mind for tonight?"

Mack laughed. "You will just have to wait and see."

Shortly after Mack and Beth left the farm, Mack noticed that the same pair of headlights stayed behind him at every turn, then left him when he turned onto the road that took him to the farm he bought that morning.

The driveway for the guesthouse wasn't plowed, but the driveway to the main house was plowed wide enough for Mack to park without being in the way.

"We're going over there," Mack told Beth as they got out of the truck. "You can wait here while I go over to turn the heat up so it warms up some inside. Then we're going to stop here for a minute. I want to tell the people who live here that it's us going in there. And I want them to meet you, so if you come here alone sometime, they know who you are."

"What did you do, Mack, rent that little house or something?"

"No, I bought this place today. Roy and Wanda are going to move here and raise beef cattle. I'll tell you all about it later."

Mack quickly walked to the guesthouse on the path Emmett had shoveled between the two houses, turned on a light, and turned the heat up.

"Now, let's go say hello to Emmett and Emma," he told Beth when he got back.

Emmett answered the door after Mack knocked and smiled when he saw who it was.

"Back so soon, Mack?" he asked.

"Well," Mack answered, "I wanted to show the guest house to my friend, Beth here. Beth, this is Emmett Schulte."

"Nice to meet you, Beth," Emmett said, taking her hand and shaking it. He turned around and said loudly, "Emma, come out here and meet Mack's friend, Beth."

Emma joined them wearing a heavy flannel robe, with her hair in curlers. "I probably shouldn't do this," she said as she joined them. "I look a fright."

"Now, Emma," Emmett said, "you couldn't look bad no matter what. You're still a good-looking woman, and we both know it. I suspect Mack does too."

"Emmett, how you talk sometimes," she answered, smiling. "Nice to meet you, Beth. We've heard about the way you're helping the Andersons. There's not many who'd do something like that nowadays."

Beth blushed. "I'm not really doing anything special. Living with them has been good for me too."

"Nonetheless, the good churchgoing folks around here have noticed. You ought to go to church with the Andersons some Sunday. There's a lot of people that would like to meet you."

"I know I should, and I will soon."

"Now that's enough of embarrassing her, Emma," Emmett said, then turned to Mack. "There's a path shoveled over to the house," he told him. "If I would've known you'd be back here so soon, I'd of plowed out the driveway for you."

"That's okay, Emmett. It's not very far to walk. I think we should be going though. It's getting late, and I don't want to keep you up too long. Beth either. She always has an early start, with chores to do and all."

Mack stepped out of the house first, and just as he did, the guesthouse exploded into flames. Mack pushed Beth back inside the house and pulled out his gun as he rushed down the steps. Two men were climbing into a pickup truck parked on the road, and Mack aimed at the one on the passenger side. For him, his aim was uncommonly good, and he hit the fleeing man in the leg, just above the knee he was trying to hit. He continued firing at the truck as it sped away. He didn't lower his pistol until it was empty.

Beth immediately ran out of the house. She was trembling when she reached him. "Are you okay?" she asked Mack when she reached him.

"Other than being real pissed, I'm fine. I did all the shooting. One of them has a bullet in his leg, so I don't think they're going to be hard to find. I know who they are anyway."

Mack called 911 to get the fire department, then the sheriff's office, and finally Dale.

"I'll be right out there, Mack," Dale told him.

Dale got there right behind the fire department. They could only contain the fire, so the guesthouse was a total loss. All Dale could do was shake his head.

"What the hell happened this time?" he asked Mack.

"You'd think the assholes of the world would learn," Mack answered. "But they never do. The fire was started by those two goons I brought in for poaching. It's my guess they thought we were in there and were hoping to kill both Beth and me in the fire."

"How did they know you were here?"

"They followed me. I didn't think much of it because when we turned onto this road, they kept on going. When we got here, I went over to the guesthouse to turn up the heat before we stopped in to see Emmett and Emma. I left a light on."

"How would they know where you were?"

"The only thing I can think of is that Von Herter told them. He knew I bought this place, and they work for him."

"Trying to prove he's involved isn't going to be easy, Mack. Unless we catch those guys and they're willing to talk."

"I know. Let's see what happens when we catch them."

"If we catch them."

"We will, Dale. One of them has a bullet in his leg and I shot up their pickup a fair amount. Even if they get out of the county, they're going to have to find a doctor somewhere. The one with the bullet in his leg was bleeding. There's a lot of blood on the road, considering the short time it took him to get in the truck after I shot him. And I gave our guys the make and color of the truck when I called this in."

"You're probably right, Mack. Since there isn't much more I can get done around here, I think I'll head back to the office to make damn sure we're doing everything possible to catch those goons. Let's meet at the office later."

Mack and Beth stayed around until the fire department finished putting out the fire, and he had apologized to Emmett and Emma for bringing them the trouble.

"That's crazy," Emmett told him. "You apologizing to us because someone tried to burn you out in a house you own. It wasn't no way your fault."

"Still, I did bring the trouble here."

"No, Mack, those bums did. Now you take Miss Beth home. She's the one who needs worrying about now. She knows what would have happened if you would have been inside when the fire started."

"You're right, Emmett. I guess I better do that."

Beth was pale and somewhat shaky when they left. Mack drove straight to the Anderson farm. They were both quiet until just before they got there.

"I hope, Mack," she said then, "that you're not blaming yourself for what happened. I want you to know that I'm certainly not blaming you."

"Well, I do blame myself to some extent. I should have been paying closer attention to what was going on with those headlights behind us."

"You know, in some ways, that would have upset me almost as much as what happened. At least now I know that I can distract you a little."

"A lot would be more like it, Beth. Sometimes, you distract me a whole lot."

"Good." She was still smiling when Mack dropped her off.

When Mack got to the sheriff's office, Dale was talking to a man Mack had no time for. Ralph Saxton had recently started as an assistant district attorney for Hall County. He hated Mack and was constantly looking for a way to get him fired.

Mack turned to leave. The last thing he was in the mood for was dealing with someone he considered to be both corrupt and incompetent.

"And just where the hell do you think you're going, Thomas?" Saxton yelled.

"Out, to help find the two men who tried to commit a double murder tonight."

"You can forget that. Now get your ass over here!"

"We already caught them, Mack," Dale said. "They're both under guard at the hospital. You hit both of them when you shot at their truck. Their wounds were only serious enough so they needed patching up."

"Not for long," Saxton told them. "You are the one who is going to be spending a long time in jail, Thomas. Sheriff Magee is locking you up now for the attempted murder of both the men you put in the hospital."

"Not hardly," Dale told him. "I don't know where you think you're coming from, Ralph, but I'm damn sure not going to arrest Mack for shooting the men who tried to kill him and Beth Cheman tonight."

"You damn sure are. I know those men, and there's no way they'd ever be involved in anything like you're accusing them of. Furthermore, Thomas here has a history of shooting people and arresting people just because he doesn't like them. So you will lock him up, Sheriff, or I will have your job before this night is over."

Mack didn't even bother to answer the man. He knew there was no way Saxton could prove anything he said.

Dale, however, did something very unlike him. He blew up. Slamming his fist into Ralph Paxton's chest, he said, "Listen, you shyster son of a bitch, don't ever come into my office threatening me or one of my deputies again." He poked Paxton again, even harder this time. "You do and your life is going to be turned into the kind of misery you can't even imagine. Now haul your sorry ass out of here and put together a case that will convict those two. You let them off, and you damn well will regret it."

"You can't talk to me that way, Magee!"

Dale slammed him again. "I just did, now get the hell out of here. And if you let those assholes off, I will have your job and your license to practice law."

Paxton threw an arm in Mack's direction, "But he—"

"But he," Dale said, slamming Paxton three more times in the chest, "is just the best damn law enforcement officer in this county. Now get the hell out of here before you really piss me off."

Paxton finally marched out the door.

"Do you have any idea, Mack," Dale asked him, "why that man hates you the way he does?"

"A couple. One, we made him and his client, Gary Brown, look like a couple of fools back when we were investigating the murder of

Gary Brown's son. Other than that, he knows I don't even have the slightest respect for him. At best, he's incompetent. At worst, he's corrupt and he knows that I know that he's in Von Herter's pocket."

"How can you know that, Mack?"

"By who gets convicted of what and who gets the toughest sentences. Some things aren't that hard to figure out."

"You're right. I just don't see why he's so focused on you, as opposed to the rest of us."

"Because Von Herter told him to."

"I guess that makes sense. I just hope they don't go after you too hard. That radio station of Von Herter's still has a lot of influence on the locals. If they go after us hard enough, we both might be out of a job."

"That's possible, I guess, but I have enough money now to fight back. The only question is how."

"That, Mack, I have no doubt you will figure out."

CHAPTER 13

Mack's day started very bad. As always, he checked in with Dale, using his new cell phone, as he was leaving the house.

"Bad news, Mack," Dale said, "there's been an accident just south of the refuge on the county road. I'm on my way. Meet me there."

As soon as Mack got to the accident scene, he got a real bad feeling in his gut. The pickup that had rolled over at least twice looked familiar. Dale filled him in immediately.

"It's Dave Sanders, Mack. The ambulance is already on its way to the hospital with him. He's hurt bad. Real bad. But I don't think the accident is what caused the most damage. From what I could tell, the very short time I saw him, he was shot. In the chest, but I'm pretty sure the bullet went in above the heart. I want you to check over the site, especially the pickup for a bullet hole. I'm going to check on Dave at the hospital. I've already called his wife, Linda, and she's already on the way there. Unless I call and tell you otherwise, I'll meet you at the hospital when you're done here."

Mack found the bullet hole in the windshield, which was miraculously not destroyed when the truck rolled. After doing a thorough search of the entire site, including both sides of the county road, Mack found the spot where the shooter stood and fired the shot. He also found a spent shell casing from the rifle the shooter used. That alone told Mack that the shooter was an amateur. A pro wouldn't leave it behind. He handled it carefully enough so that it could be checked for fingerprints. He completed his checking of the shooting site, then left for the hospital.

Dale was talking to Linda Sanders, Dave's wife, when Mack got to the hospital. She had been crying, but now seemed remarkably calm.

"I'm so sorry, Linda," Mack told her. "Do you have any idea who would do this to Dave?"

"No. As I already told Dale, Dave just doesn't have any real enemies. Like everyone, there are people he disagrees with and who disagree with him. But nowhere is there a reason for anyone doing something like this."

"So no one has threatened you guys or anything like that?"

"Not really."

"What does not really mean"

"It means that I can't think of anything I would take seriously."

"Do you mean there is something that happened that you didn't take seriously?"

"Just a silly phone call I got a few days after I sold you the Schultz farm. Someone left me a message on my phone saying I should be more careful whom I sell to."

"That was it? Nothing else in the message?"

"He just told me to be careful whom I sold to, then hung up. I think it probably was because I've sold a few houses to some of the people connected to that Lands Magnificent bunch. A lot of people don't like that group."

"That's true," Mack said, "but that might not be what the call was about. Von Herter was extremely angry when he found out you sold the farm to me."

"Now, Mack," Dale told him, "don't jump to any conclusions. We don't have any evidence that Von Herter was behind this."

"Not yet. But this is damn sure the kind of thing he's all too often done. So let's not rule him out as a suspect."

"We won't. But we still have to look at all the possibilities."

"I don't have any argument with that, as long as Von Herter is looked at too. And regardless of who is responsible for this, if there is any chance that phone call had anything to do with what happened to Dave, it is possible that they might go after Linda too."

"Oh," Linda said, "I don't think anyone is really after me."

"Mack's right," Dale told her. "Which means we'll have to make sure you're safe."

"I'll keep an eye on her," Mack volunteered. He turned to Linda. "I'm fairly sure you're safe while you're here, but I don't want you out of here alone. Call me when you're ready to leave, and I'll come by and follow you home."

"I don't really think that's necessary," Linda argued, but it was obvious that she was pleased that he was so concerned about her.

"Maybe not, Linda," Mack told her, his tone of voice letting her know that he meant it. "But you will call me and I will follow you home. After all that's happened around here since that damn project in the refuge started, we aren't taking any chances."

"It might be late before I leave here tonight, Mack."

"I don't care what time it is. You're not leaving here alone."

"Okay, I'll call."

Dale's cell phone interrupted their conversation. "Mack and I will be there shortly," he said after a very short conversation. He looked at Mack. "We've got to go. There's been another murder."

Paul Danielson was already at the murder site, which was in a parking lot at the beginning of a snowmobile trail that made a loop around the refuge. The victim was a big male, sitting in his pickup. All of his face and a good part of his head was gone. A shotgun was on the ground, not far from the truck.

"Well," Paul said to Mack and Dale when they arrived. "We have a definite pattern. The third guy last summer had his face blown off by a shotgun. I surely do doubt that this is just a coincidence. There must be some kind of connection. Also, this guy is wearing one of those DR jackets. Which means there is a connection both with last summer's murders and that local DR club."

"I don't think you'll get any disagreement from either one of us," Dale said.

"But who the hell could it be that's doing these murders?" Mack wandered aloud, while at the same time, knowing who he had to check on, even though he was sure that the person he would be checking on was very unlikely to be the murderer.

When Mack left the hospital, he drove directly to the Bob Anderson farm. He needed to talk to James Anderson, Bob's father. Unknown to the police in Minneapolis, James was responsible for the two shotgun deaths that occurred the previous summer that Paul Danielson was concerned about. Who did the killing, with the knife to the throat of the victim, was not known. James did know but didn't and wouldn't say who it was.

When he got to the farm, James was not feeling well and was in bed.

"His heart is acting up," Bob told Mack. "He's been in bed for the past couple of days. If it isn't real important, it would be best if you could wait until he's feeling better before you talk to him."

"It's not important," Mack told him, knowing now that James had nothing to do with the latest murder. "I was just curious if he had any ideas about who would try to kill Dave Sanders. Have you got any ideas, Bob?"

"Not really. Dave isn't the kind of man anyone is likely to go gunning for."

"I don't think so either. But someone does."

After Mack left the farm, he met Dale and Paul at Katie's Kafe for lunch.

"I think the best way to deal with the murders and the attempted murder," Dale said, "is to put one of you in charge of each case. Mack, I want you to handle the attempt on Dave Sanders. Paul, you take the lead on the other three murders. But go ahead and work together when it's appropriate."

"That sounds okay to me," Paul said. "But first I have a couple of questions." He looked at Dale first, then Mack. "Is there anyone in this area that you can think of that was in anyway involved in all that happened with so-called home for girls last summer that I could talk to? I have no doubts at all that there was a connection between what happened then and the three murders."

"Lisa Anderson is the only one I can think of right now, but I can absolutely guarantee she had nothing to do with any of this,"

Mack said, knowing he would never tell Paul or even Dale, that James Anderson, Lisa's grandfather, was the one who committed the two shotgun murders that occurred then.

"No one else that you can think of then?"

"No, I don't think…" It was then that Mack suddenly remembered that Lisa's friend Terry Holstrom was one of the girls there. "Sorry, Paul, I forgot. There is one other person. She was one of the girls there. And much longer than Lisa."

"Is there any way you can set it up for me to talk to her?"

Mack checked his watch. "I can do better than that, Paul. Lisa has organized a group trying to save the rest of the refuge. She, Terry, and another girl will be having a meeting of sorts at the high school in a few minutes. If we leave now, we will be able to join them and have an informal conversation with them. Also, I just remembered. Terry has red hair."

"How old is she?"

"I don't know for sure, but she's in some of Lisa Anderson's classes, and Lisa is sixteen. So I'd guess the Terry's either the same age or close anyway."

"Well then, Mack, let's go talk to those girls."

CHAPTER 14

LISA AND HER FRIENDS WERE surprised to see Mack again and even more surprised to see that he brought along someone they didn't know.

"Why are you here, Mack?" Lisa asked even before Mack and Paul had the chance to sit down. "And who is this man with you?"

"First," Mack asked, "is it okay if we sit down?"

"Of course it's okay."

"Good." Mack and Paul sat down with the girls. "This gentleman with me today is a detective. He is working with the sheriff's department to help us solve the recent murders of the three men who were probable members of that DR club. We are hoping one of you might know something more about the club or the men who were murdered."

"There's nothing new that I can tell you, Mack," Lisa said right away, then introduced herself and Jo and Terry to Paul.

"I don't know if it means anything," Jo said after the introduction, "but my cousin Skip finally told me that the real name of the club is Deer Runners."

"Deer Runners," Mack said. "Really? For sure?"

"Well, I don't know for absolute sure," Jo said. "Only what my cousin Skip said."

"Oh, I'm not at all doubting what you're saying. And it does explain a lot of what is going on around here lately."

"So what are we supposed to be able to tell you about some murders?" Terry asked. "Do you guys think we did them or something?"

The question surprised both Paul and Mack, and they both just stared at her for a few moments. That was when Mack noticed a slight discoloration in Terry's upper arm. The top she wore had short sleeves, and a part of her arm, between the sleeve and her elbow, was healing from a recent bruise. He didn't want to say anything in front of the girls, so he answered Terry with an "of course not" and told Paul, "I think these kids have helped us a lot just coming up with the name of the club. So let's let them get on with their meeting."

Mack left the table. "Thanks for your help," he told the girls.

Paul still had some questions he wanted to ask but took the hint from Mack that they should leave and followed his lead.

When they reached Mack's pickup, Paul finally asked, "So are you going to tell me what that was about? There was a lot more we could have asked them."

"I know," Mack agreed with a heavy sigh. "But I think we have a suspect now, and I thought we should talk about it before we go any further with more questions."

"Are you sure about that, Mack?" Paul asked, somewhat surprised by Mack's comment. "Which one?"

"Terry."

"Why do you think it's Terry, Mack?"

"Three things. One, the question about us thinking they did the murders. Two, she has a bruise on her arm that looks like it goes up higher, like maybe to her shoulder. A shotgun could do that, especially a young girl. And third, she went through pure hell for a fairly long time. That could make her crazy enough to do something this radical."

"Jesus, Mack, you got me hired as a consultant to solve those murders, and I think you just did it. That's some good detective work. The thing is, though, I've kind of been wondering about her already. I need to check her out. I need to find everything I can about her before we can make any moves."

"You're right, so I'm going to bring you back to the station now, and I'm going to see what I can find out about the Dave Thomas shooting."

"I can't argue with that, Mack. Especially after what we've figured out today."

CHAPTER 15

MACK SPENT THE REST OF the day in a fruitless search for
Dave Sanders's attempted murderer. He got home just in
time for supper. Roy picked up on his somber mood as
soon as they sat down at the table.

"Something bothering you, Mack?" Roy immediately asked.

"Just the usual," Mack answered. "Murders and attempted
murders."

"Are you being serious or sarcastic?"

"Serious. There's been three recent murders and today an
attempted murder. And the attempted murder was someone we
know, have done business with, and like. Dave Sanders."

"Who the hell would want to kill a decent guy like him? You
got any ideas?"

"Just one. Von Herter."

"Why do you think it was him?"

"He's the only one stupid enough to want to kill someone for
so little reason. And he's the only one to threaten Dave or his wife,
Linda. After she sold the land to me, land Von Herter wanted, she
got a call telling her to be careful who she sold to. He really wanted
the land, and the call was made after I shoved the fact I bought the
land in his face."

"Maybe you shouldn't have done that, Mack, given what a nut-
case he is. That aside, do you have proof it was him?"

"Not yet, but this time, I do plan to get some. My major goal right now is to rid this county of Eric Von Herter."

"Why do you think you'll be able to do that this time when you couldn't before?"

"Because this time, I'll be able to concentrate on just this case. Paul Danielson, our new detective, will be handling the murders. And that we made easier today because we have a suspect."

Before Roy could ask another question, Mack's cell phone rang. It was Linda Sanders.

"Dave is out for the night," she said. "So I'm ready to go home now. You said to call, and I did."

"I'm at home, so it'll take a bit for me to get there, but I'd appreciate it if you'd wait for me. I really don't think it would be a good idea for you to be out there alone this time of the night."

"I'll wait."

"That was Linda Sanders," Mack explained. "I'm going to follow her home to make sure she gets there safely."

No one argued with him, and he left for the hospital immediately. Linda was waiting for him at the entrance when he got there. He drove her to her car, then followed her out of the parking lot. It was a quiet ride on the county road until they were about a mile from the turnoff to her home. Then, suddenly, a speeding pickup passed Mack, then swerved into Linda's car, spinning her car a half circle before it slid into the ditch, leaving her side of the car away from the pickup.

The pickup skidded to a stop and someone leaped out of the passenger side. Whoever it was had a gun in their hand. Mack was quickly out of his truck, but the man with the gun fired first. He grazed Mack's left arm, just below the shoulder, and Mack fired back three times, hitting him with every shot. He went down face first and lay still. Then Mack turned his weapon on the truck and fired three more times at the driver's side. The pickup jumped ahead, but just as quickly stopped. The man in the driver's seat opened the door, then fell out of the truck.

Mack checked to be sure Linda was okay first. Finding that she was, he checked on the two men from the pickup. The one in the ditch was dead, but the one lying in the middle of the road still had a pulse. He called for an ambulance, then Dale. While he waited, he went back to Linda.

"Are you okay, Linda?" he asked.

"I don't know. I'm too scared to know. That guy who was shooting at you, was he going to shoot me?"

"That would be my guess. They likely would have tried if your car would have stopped with your door facing them instead of away from them. That's what forced them to shoot at me first. I am damn sure glad that you called me. If I hadn't been behind you, well..."

That's when Linda noticed the blood streaming from Mack's shoulder.

"My god, Mack," she cried, "you're shot. Are you going to be okay?"

"I'll be okay," he told her. "I don't think it's a serious wound."

The ambulance arrived a few minutes later. The man in the street was still alive, but barely. Linda grabbed the man from the ambulance as soon as he got out, forcing him to check Mack's wound. The ambulance driver checked the other two. After patching up Mack's arm, the man went to assist the driver.

Dale arrived a few minutes later. "Are you sure you really needed to shoot as many times as you did, Mack?" he asked.

"Yes, I am. They were both armed, and I didn't see much sense in getting shot a second time. Also, it's pretty damn obvious that Linda would be dead now if I wouldn't have been here."

"I know. It's just that there will be a really big deal made out of this. So I might be forced to put you on suspension."

"No, Dale, I don't think so. I don't care a damn how big a deal Von Herter tries to make out of it. Because if he tries to push it too hard, I will sue him. And anybody else who tries to push too hard. I don't have to win to beat them if I make it expensive enough for them. So there will be no suspension. You need to keep me working so that this time Von Herter really does go down."

"But, Mack..."

"No, Dale, not this time. If getting shot and saving Linda's life doesn't justify my shooting the way I did, then too goddamn bad. We no longer have to do Von Herter's bidding. If you suspend me, I'll quit. I'm not going to put up with any of that kind of bullshit this time. This time, Von Herter is going down."

"You'd really quit."

"Damn right. So now, let me take Linda home. I think she's had enough for one day."

"You're right, Mack. About all of it. There's plenty of support on the way, so go ahead and take her home. She's definitely had enough for one day. When the tow truck gets here, I'll have them haul her car to town to be checked out."

Linda was still visibly shaken when Mack helped her into his pickup. She took his hand when he got in, sliding over next to him.

"I'm still scared and cold now," she said, "so if you don't mind, I'd like to ride next to you."

"I don't mind, and I don't blame you for being scared. What happened to you tonight should never happen to anyone."

"When you were talking to Dale, you blamed what happened on Eric Von Herter. Do you really think he was the one responsible?"

"I don't think so, Linda. I know so. He's done this kind of thing all too often. But this time, he's not going to get away with it."

"How are you going to prove he was the one?"

"I don't know yet, but I will. One way or the other, I will."

When they got to Linda's, Mack called Ben, told him what happened without mentioning that he'd been shot, and that he was staying the night at Linda's. He wasn't about to leave her, even if Theresa was there. He was the one with a gun, and he was the one who knew how to use it.

CHAPTER 16

IT WAS A CLEAR NIGHT, so he had no trouble finding what he was looking for. He had a heavy-duty bolt cutter with him, and he made short work of the small lock on the door of the small tin building. But he was careful enough with the lock so it would take a close look to see that it had been cut after he replaced it on the door.

He had gone on the internet since his first visit, so he knew what explosives to look for. He loaded more than he needed onto his snowmobile, then got on his machine and headed back home. Once there, he stowed all the explosives in a previously prepared spot. He was ready now. Ready to show everyone that he could do a lot more than shoot some deer or even start some silly rally. What he had planned was much bigger. He'd prove to those Deer Runners and those three girls just how much he could do all alone.

He was smiling when he went to bed that night.

CHAPTER 17

THERESA WAS ALREADY IN BED and asleep when they got to Linda's. It was Mack's intention to sleep in his clothes on Linda's couch that night. She would have none of it. She was relentless.

When he told her that he'd be just fine on the couch, she said, "No! No, you won't. You saved my life tonight and got shot doing it. The least I can do is make sure you're comfortable."

Since he and her husband Dave were close to the same size, she gave him a pair of Dave's pajamas to wear. Then she ran a bathtub of water and insisted he use it. "In order to sleep comfortable," she said. She was determined that he was going to be comfortable while sleeping in her house. Once in the tub, she joined him in the bathroom.

"I know this is a bit embarrassing," she told him, "but I also know how hard it will be for you to wash with that bandage on your arm."

So she used a wash cloth to bath him everywhere except those parts that would have been very embarrassing. Her hands were soft and caressing, as she moved the cloth over his body, almost the way a lover would. Mack noticed but let it go. She turned her back when he got out of the tub but helped him use the towel on his back, legs, and feet.

By then, Mack was surprised and somewhat disturbed by the attention she was giving him. He was getting what he considered too much pleasure from all the attention, so he was beginning to feel guilty. After she got Mack settled on the couch in the living room, Linda used the shower and put on a nightgown. He had a hard time believing his eyes when she returned.

She was wearing a red silk-like nightgown. It wasn't particularly revealing, but it fit her perfectly and highlighted every feminine curve of her body. Without knowing it, no one would have been able to guess her age. Standing before him, she was one of the most beautiful women he had ever seen.

He shook his head, smiled, and said, "Wow."

She smiled back. "That's as good a compliment as I've ever gotten, Mack. It's really nice to be wowed at any time, but especially at my age."

"I don't care what your age is, Linda. You are a very beautiful woman."

"Well, thank you again. Now, can I get you anything? A beer or maybe a glass of wine?"

"Well, I appreciate the offer, but I'm fine for now."

"Okay, but I'd like to have a glass of wine. Do you mind staying up with me for a while? I'd like to talk a little too. I'm still a bit unnerved by all that's happened today. Or are you too tired to stay up any longer. If you are, I've already turned down the covers on the bed in the guest room."

"I don't mind staying up for a while. It's been a rough day for me too. And I guess I will have a glass of wine. Something very dry if you have it."

Linda left, then returned with a glass of ice-cold, very dry white wine.

"I hope this is what you're looking for," she said as she handed it to him, letting her hand brush his as she did.

He tasted the wine, then agreed with her.

"It is," he said, pretending not to notice her hand as it moved across his.

She sat down on the couch, surprising him when she sat down in the middle, rather than the other end from where he was sitting. She turned to him and smiled.

"I hope," she said, "I'm not making you uncomfortable sitting next to you. But after all that's happened today, I'm feeling a little insecure. And I am sure, that if you weren't here, I'd be just plain scared."

"You go ahead and sit wherever you feel the most comfortable, Linda. Because I do understand how you must feel right now after the day you've had."

"How about you, Mack? How are you feeling now? You haven't had what anyone would call an easy day. You've gone through a lot. Not only were you shot, but you were forced to shoot someone just to save my life."

"That's still not much compared to what you've gone through."

"Well, I think it is," she said as she moved closer to him, then leaned against him. "And I can't even begin to tell you how much I appreciate you staying here tonight. There's something about you, Mack Thomas, that makes me feel not only more secure, but that the world is a better place with you in it. I really am terribly worried about Dave and whether he's going to recover or how well he'll recover if he does. With you being here right now, it makes me feel as though no matter what happens, it'll be a little less bad."

She took his hand and moved his arm around her shoulders.

"Now please hold me," she said. "Just hold me for a while."

He did, and she snuggled even closer, then lifted her head and kissed him. Without thinking, acting on some instinct and a real but deeply buried desire, Mack returned the kiss with passion.

Just as his hand moved to her breasts, they were interrupted.

Theresa joined them in the living room.

"I'm sorry," she said, "for interrupting you guys, but I'm having trouble sleeping. I'll go back to bed if you want me to."

"No," Linda told her, "you weren't interrupting anything."

"Are you sure?"

"You're fine," Mack told her.

"I'll get you a glass of wine," Linda said. When she returned with it, she handed it to Theresa, who was sitting on the opposite end of the couch from Mack. Linda then sat down on the love seat across from the couch.

The three of them made small talk for an hour before they all decided it was time for bed.

Mack lay in bed, wide awake, for about half an hour, thinking about what had occurred between him and Linda. As much as he had desired her, he was relieved that it hadn't gone any further.

His relief was short-lived however, because the door to his room opened, then closed very quietly. Linda joined him, making no pretense about what she wanted.

Mack, being who he was, felt guilty as he took her in his arms. But this time, it would take more than guilt to...

CHAPTER 18

THE GUILT MACK FELT WHEN he woke up the next morning was far less than he thought it would be when he fell asleep the night before. What happened between him and Linda was something he would never have believed could happen, but given the circumstances, it no longer seemed to be something that was out of place or wrong. He was sure it would never have happened under any other circumstances, and that it would never happen again, but he couldn't summon up any regrets that it had.

Linda gave him a wide smile when he finished in the bathroom and joined her in the kitchen.

"I know," she told him, "that given everything that happened yesterday, I shouldn't be able to smile this morning. But you, Mack Thomas, could probably make just about any woman smile the next morning. Also, just so the guilt I'm sure you feel right now isn't too strong, I have to tell you something about Dave and I. We have had a special kind of relationship for a very long time. So please don't feel guilty about him. If he knew, he would understand better than anyone else ever would or could."

"Thank you for telling me that, Linda. If anything could make me feel guilty, it would be Dave."

"Now, I would appreciate it if you never tell anyone what I just told you."

"I won't, any more than I would ever tell anyone anything about what happened. And that's not because I have any regrets. I don't."

"Now that that is settled, what are your plans for the day?"

"The first thing I'm going to do is give you a ride to the hospital. Then…"

"You don't have to do that, Mack. I still know how to drive."

Mack sighed heavily, but smiled when he did. "After all that happened yesterday, you should be the first to understand why I can't let you drive or go anywhere alone right now. Not to mention that your car isn't even here. It's in town."

"Oh my god, how could I forget that? And I do understand your concern, Mack. It's just that I'm not at all used to this kind of thing."

"Hopefully, Linda, it won't last too much longer."

Linda chuckled. "Well, there are parts of this arrangement that I wouldn't mind keeping. At least for a while."

Mack was somewhat surprised by her comment and wasn't sure how to respond. So he just smiled.

Linda understood his not answering, and to show him that she did, she kissed him. A long and very passionate kiss. Mack totally responded to it.

"That was nice," Linda said, as they broke the kiss. She waited a moment, then returned the smile Mack gave her. "I guess," she said when Mack let her go and stepped back, "I should tell Theresa that we're leaving now."

Theresa was still in bed, so Linda woke her to tell her that they were leaving for the hospital.

"Already," Theresa said. "I wanted to go along."

"It's going to be a very long day," Linda told her. "And I won't be able to take you home if you get tired. My car is in town in the garage getting checked out and repaired if it needs anything."

"After all you've done for me, Linda, staying with you at the hospital is the least I can do. So if you don't mind waiting while I get dressed, I do want to go with you."

"Okay, if you hurry, we'll wait."

When she returned, before she told Mack that they were going to wait for Theresa, Linda walked up to Mack, wrapped her arms around his neck, and kissed him again.

"That," she said, "was just something I wanted to do."

"I'm glad you did" was Mack's only answer.

CHAPTER 19

Just as the three of them were about to enter the hospital, Eric Von Herter and a large burly man came out of the hospital. Von Herter stopped and glared at them.

"Well," he snarled at them, "what do you know. If it isn't the county whore and her bitch sister." He focused on Linda. "So what are you doing now, bitch, fucking Thomas here just because he bought that farm and got you a big commission. Your almost dead husband is going to love to hear that when I tell him about your whoring around."

Linda quickly moved close to Von Herter and moved her right hand back as if she was going to slap him. Instead, she grabbed her heavy hand-crafted leather purse from her shoulder. With all the strength in her body, which was considerable considering that she worked out on a regular basis, she swung the purse at Von Herter. It made a distinct thump when it connected to the side of his head.

Von Herter screamed and staggered back, but still managed to grab Linda's arm. He brought his fist back to hit her, but before he could, Theresa jumped on his back, reached around, and buried her sharp fingernails in his face. He tried to shake free, but that only raked her nails across his skin, leaving deep bloody scratches on both sides of his face.

The big man with Von Herter moved to assist him. Before he could, Mack had his pistol out and from behind, buried it in the back of his head.

"Move another inch," Mack told him, "and I will happily blow a nice big hole in your head."

"Tough guy, huh," the big man growled. "You wouldn't be so tough if you didn't have that gun in your hand."

"You're probably right," Mack agreed. "But the point right now, I do have the gun and I will use it if I need to. So get face down on the ground before I'm forced to blow that great big hole in your ugly head."

The big man did what he was told to do as he realized that Mack wasn't kidding. Then Mack turned to the battle between the two women and Von Herter. He did it just in time to see Linda land one more heavy blow to the top of Von Herter's head with her solidly built leather purse. Since Von Herter didn't have any fight left in him, Mack called a halt to the proceedings. Then he immediately handcuffed Von Herter.

It was difficult for Mack to keep from laughing. Theresa had left a number of deep scratch marks on his face, and there were several visible bruises from Linda's purse.

"Are you sure I can't just kill him?" Linda asked. "I'd sure like to."

"So would I," Theresa agreed.

"No, I don't think I can let you. Not this time anyway. I'm still a deputy sheriff, otherwise I might not just let you, I might encourage you to do it."

"So," Linda asked, "are you going to arrest all of us or just Von Herter?"

"Only Von Herter and his pal down there on the ground."

"Can you really do that?" Linda asked. "I hit him first."

"No, Linda, you didn't. I distinctly saw him grab your arm first. You were only defending yourself. Then Theresa assisted you when she feared for your life. Isn't that right, Theresa?"

Theresa gave Mack a big smile. "That's right, Mack. That is exactly what happened."

"But, Mack…" Linda started to say, but Mack quickly interrupted her.

"That is what happened, Linda. Yesterday, he tried to have your husband murdered, then tried to have you murdered. He's guilty of every crime a human being could commit, so please don't say anything to anyone that contradicts what Theresa and I just said. There comes a time when enough is definitely enough."

"Okay, Mack. I won't argue with you. He did grab me first."

"Good, now why don't you go get someone from the hospital to bandage this asshole before I haul his sorry ass off to jail? And while you do that, I'm going to give Dale a call."

Dale was only a couple of minutes away, so he arrived even before a doctor got to Von Herter.

Mack immediately told Dale to cuff the big guy, so he could relax. He was smart enough to know, that if it came to it, fighting with him would be a totally losing proposition, and he really didn't want to shoot anyone else that day. The shootings the day before were a lot more than he had ever wanted to be involved in.

"What the hell did you do to Von Herter? He looks like you beat the living hell out of him. Did you use your pistol on him or something?"

"No, Dale, I never touched him."

"That's right," Theresa, who was standing right there, told Dale. "Mack never touched him. He tried to hurt Linda, and she defended herself. I was afraid that he might kill her, so I helped her. I gave him the scratches."

"So where is Linda now?"

"She went to get a doctor to look at Von Asshole here. They just came out of the hospital now."

"So what have we got here?" the doctor asked. He obviously knew who Von Herter was, and the tone of his voice showed that he wasn't overly concerned about the man.

"It's what you would call," Mack said, this time being unsuccessful at hiding his grin, "the result of the wrong man assaulting the wrong woman."

"Really? Well I suppose I should have a look at him." The doctor made a quick check of Von Herter, then turned to Mack and Dale. "None of his injuries look bad enough to keep him in the hospital," he decided, "but you should bring him inside so I can bandage him up some. Are you going to let him go or arrest him?"

"I am definitely arresting him and his pal here," Mack explained. "Linda, Theresa, and I will all be filing assault charges against him and his pissant friend here."

While they helped the doctor get Von Herter into the hospital, Dale loaded up the big man into his squad car and left for the police station to lock him up.

About an hour later, Mack met Dale there. They locked Von Herter in a cell as far from the man he had been with as they could.

"Are you sure," Dale asked Mack, "that Von Herter grabbed Linda first? Joe Tubbs, the guy who was there, swears that Linda hit him first."

"He can swear all he wants. Von Herter started it. All three of us are going to file assault charges tonight, after I pick them up at the hospital. So make sure everything is ready for us to sign when we get here. As far as Joe goes, he tried to draw his gun on me. I just beat him to it. So before you get any ideas about me being too hard on him, just remember that I would have been justified in shooting him."

"I know, Mack," Dale told him, "But I hope you realize that his lawyer will have them both out by tomorrow."

"It doesn't matter. They're going to have to make a court appearance sometime, and we will all be there when they do. Von Herter is not going to walk away totally free on this one or anything else I catch him doing. Who knows what else I might come up with to hold against him."

"That sounds like you have a vendetta against him."

"Good, because that's exactly what I have. So how is Paul doing on the three murders?"

"I think I'll let him tell you that. He just walked in."

Paul was glad to see that Mack was there because then he could tell both him and Dale at the same time what he had learned about Terry Holstrom.

"She was definitely one of the girls being held and used for prostitution at that home for girls that Genesis Paul was running," Paul said, referring to the evangelical preacher who had started his own church, along with several homes for young girls. "But she wasn't one of the girls we found there after the murders took place. We don't know why, we just know she wasn't. I haven't found any record of her being a patient, with any doctor or clinic that deals with the kind of trauma she went through, around here or in or near Minneapolis where she lived before her and her father moved up here."

"Do you really think though," Dale asked, "that she's a viable suspect?"

"Yes and no. I do think that it's possible she could be capable of killing the kind of men who were murdered, after what she must have gone through. Especially since she apparently hasn't had any help or treatment for it. But without telling him my reasons for asking, I checked with her father about her staying out late at night. He claimed that she always came home at a reasonable hour. The problem there is, he seemed a little too nervous for someone who was telling the truth."

"What do you suggest we do then?"

"Other than let me continue to look into those murders, nothing for now. I also checked into all three of the men who were murdered. None of them have ever been arrested in this county, but they all have records of one kind or another out of Minnesota. And all three came here to work for Eric Von Herter. They definitely were not nice people. So if while I check things out, there are any more murders, it probably won't be anyone whose death will leave any great loss to humanity in general. Mostly, they are the same kind of people who did to Terry what they did."

"I think you're probably right about that," Mack agreed, knowing the kind of people Von Herter hired. "Sometimes, it gets hard to care much, if at all, about creatures like that."

Before they could talk any more about the murders, Mack's cell phone rang. It was Lisa Anderson, and he turned his back on Paul and Dale to hear her better. She gave Mack some very interesting news. He listened intently as she talked, then grinned broadly when the conversation ended and he turned back to face Dale and Paul.

"You must have just gotten some really good news," Dale commented. "Given that big grin on your face."

"I did," Mack said, looking Dale in the eye. "It was actually great news for me, but I'm not sure how you're going to take it."

"Why would I not like news that you consider great?"

"Because of what I fully intend to do about it."

"I don't think I like the sound of that, Mack. What is this all about and what do you intend to do about whatever it is?"

"That was Lisa Anderson on the phone. She just learned from Skip Halbertson what the Deer Runners have planned for tonight. What they do is go into the refuge at night. This time of the year on snowmobile and find deer to run down. They find it great fun to run the deer to complete exhaustion, then cut their throats. According to Skip, they're planning a run tonight."

"And you plan on doing something about it?"

"I do, Dale. I'm going to round up as many people as I can, and we are going to into the refuge after them, catch as many of them as we can, and arrest them. Plan on having some full jail cells before the night is over."

'Who do you think is going to be willing to help you with something like that?" Dale asked, sounding like he didn't believe anyone would.

"The first one who'll volunteer when I tell him about it will be Rich Hayden, the manager of the refuge. My uncle Roy and Wanda will. Maybe even Dad. People like Linda Sanders and her sister Teresa. Dan Locks, the principal of the high school, might help. A lot of people like that. And maybe even some of your other deputies. Every one of them is tired of this kind of bullshit."

"You know what, Mack," Paul said, "I think I'd like to be part of it too, if I could ride with someone."

"You can ride with me," Dale told him. "Mack's right. We're all way past letting any more of this kind of crap continue. Like you, Mack, I'm going in with my pickup. The snow still isn't deep enough to slow it down much, and we'll need more than one vehicle to haul the prisoners to jail."

Mack's first call was to Linda to explain what was going on and that he thought it would be a good idea if she and Theresa were a part of it.

"Not only," he explained, "because I think you'll actually be safer there than at home alone, but that you'll be an asset to the proceedings. The more people involved, the better."

Linda and Theresa weren't just willing, they were excited about going.

Mack and Dale both made several calls and managed to raise a large number of people to assist in the raid on the Deer Runners. Rich Hayden, manager of the refuge, loved the idea and agreed to put together a plan of action. Everyone agreed to meet at the refuge headquarters at ten p.m., which was a couple of hours earlier than the DRs were planning their deer run.

Mack left the station then and drove to the Anderson dairy farm. He wanted to talk to Beth. She greeted him when he got there, and because Lisa was still in school, she wrapped her arms around his neck and kissed him.

He responded to her but felt uneasy about it. And he knew that what he was feeling was caused by the guilt over what happened the night before. For Mack, no matter what the circumstances were, no matter that what he did wasn't really going to hurt anyone, it would as so many other things did, leave him feeling a bit guilty for his own imperfections.

"So what brings you here this time of the day?"

"Mostly, I wanted to see you. Until Von Herter's men tried to kill Dave Sanders and then Linda, I had planned to take you out to eat or something. And the way things are now, it's going to be a while before I can get free. So I stopped now mostly just to see you."

"You said mostly. What's the other reason?"

"To tell you about tonight. That gang we've all been wondering about turned out to be called the Deer Runners." Mack went on to tell Beth about the plans for the night.

"So you've got a whole bunch of people lined up to catch as many of them in the act of running down deer so you can arrest them?"

"That's right."

"I want to go along. I hate those people. Killing innocent animals just for sport is evil no matter how someone does it. Killing them that way, well, it goes so far beyond any kind of decency that I can't describe it."

"I'd love to have you there, Beth, but I already have two people riding with me in my pickup."

"I assumed that, Mack, given that you're still guarding Linda and Theresa." She grinned at him. "But Bob has snowmobiles, and I'm sure he'll let me borrow one of them. Who knows, he might even come along."

"That sounds great. And I hate to tell you this, but I've got to go. There's lots of places to be and people to see. Dad, Roy, and Wanda being first on the list."

"I understand," she said. "I'll see you tonight." She kissed him goodbye, and he left for home.

Everyone was surprised to see him when he got there. Then he was surprised when Wanda greeted him with a hug and a kiss. It was beginning to feel real strange, having so many beautiful women kiss him so thoroughly on the same day.

Roy spoke first, "What brings you home in the middle of the day?"

Mack explained the situation to them. When he finished, Roy had a big grin on his face, as did Wanda. Ben's look was more serious, but not at all negative about what Mack just told them.

"It sure looks like Roy is going to enjoy himself tonight," Wanda said. "I think I'll have some fun myself because I damn sure will be there with Roy."

"Count me in on it too," Ben said. "It'll feel good to see a bunch of the world's assholes all go to jail at the same time."

"Good," Mack said. "So how do you all plan to ride out in the refuge?"

"My pickup has four-wheel drive," Ben said. "So the three of us can ride together."

"No need for that, Ben," Roy told him. "My truck isn't four-wheel drive, but it is high clearance and I have chains for it. I get one hell of a lot of traction with them on the dual wheels in the back. Not to mention, there's not enough snow cover to slow those of us in trucks down that much."

"Good. And that way, Dad's got an open seat if there's anyone who needs a ride."

And Mack already knew who that person was going to be. He knew that his father really wanted to see Theresa Lorring again, but just didn't know how to go about arranging it. This way, though, if they were thrown together for just a little while, there would be no expectations on either of their parts. It was a good way to let nature take its course.

Mack left the kitchen then and started making phone calls. He was determined to get as much help as possible for the raid on the Deer Runners as he could.

CHAPTER 29

People began arriving at the refuge's headquarters as early as nine p.m. By ten, there were six four-wheel-drive pickups along with Roy's one-ton truck and over two dozen snowmobiles. Mack was pleased to see that Bob Anderson was there with Beth, as were Dan Locks and a couple of teachers. Four of the deputies made it. More would have come, but some were on duty and others would be by the time the raid started. Dale and Paul were the first to arrive, except for Mack. Rich Hayden was still there after putting in a very long day.

When Ben arrived, Mack immediately brought Theresa over to his truck. He hadn't told either one of them about his plan and wasn't even sure it was going to work. If either one of them objected, that would be the end of it. Much to Mack's surprise, they both just smiled when Theresa climbed into Ben's truck.

Mack breathed a sigh of relief, then joined Rich and Dale, who were starting to organize everyone according to the plan they had worked out. As they gathered everyone around to assign positions and issue final instructions, they answered any and all questions.

The plan was simple. Everyone would spread out around the lake, under whatever cover they could find along the shore. As they moved into position, they drove their machines along the shoreline so that they didn't leave any tracks in the middle of the lake because they were sure that the Deer Runners would come that way. Rich made sure everyone knew the various locations where the deer were yarded up, so the animals wouldn't be disturbed ahead of time.

With the plan they had, no one worried much about the tracks they did leave. The men and boys that were part of the Deer Runners were way too arrogant to ever think anyone could catch them. After all, most of them came from families who could provide them with the fastest and most powerful snowmobiles money could buy. They also considered themselves to be among the best snowmobile drivers anywhere.

Mack and Dale were each stationed at either end of the posse they had formed. One of the deputies was stationed in the middle. The three of them were driving pickups equipped with flashing lights and sirens. The signal to move in on the deer killers would come from Dale when he turned on his lights and sirens. He would decide when they had actually committed a crime they could be arrested for. Mack and the other deputy would immediately turn theirs on, and then the entire posse would attempt to surround the killers.

The plan didn't work near as well as they had hoped when it jumped into action, but the results were far superior to anything they had expected. Everyone's timing was a bit off, as they charged out of their positions, which added to the confusion that followed.

All of the big and brave deer murderers panicked the instant the lights and sirens came on. It was total chaos as those who thought they were superior to most everyone else flipped their machines in their panic. Others ran into trees or each other. Many of them simply gave up when they were actually surrounded. If they were riding double and the rider fell off, none of the drivers stopped to pick up their fallen companion. For the mighty Deer Runners, it was totally each person for themselves.

Of those who managed to break away, Roy chased one of the adults in the group to the far side of the lake where Roy forced him into a patch of woods too thick to drive a snowmobile. When Roy got out of his truck to deal with the man, he took a swing at Roy. That was a big mistake. He was unconscious when Roy brought him to the headquarters where they were gathering together all of those who thought they were going to have a big night of fun torturing deer. Deer who certainly had far more value to humanity and the planet earth than they ever had.

Mack chased another man who was a known bodyguard for Von Herter. He didn't attack Mack though. He broke both his arms when he flipped his machine trying to get away by climbing a steep ditch by the road. A large rock hidden under the snow was the culprit that did it. Broken arms or not, Mack was none too gentle when he loaded the man into the back of his truck.

"There was a time," Linda said when he got back in the truck, "that I would have thought you were too hard on that guy. Not any-more. After seeing what they were trying to do to that poor little deer, I'd like to rip that bastard's eyes out."

"So would I," Mack agreed. "So would I." Then he leaned over and kissed Linda in a way that she surely knew that she'd been kissed. "And I only did that," he told her, "because I very much wanted to do it."

She simply responded with a smile. A very big smile.

That made Mack wonder at all the strange turns that can develop in a person's life, as he drove back to the refuge headquarters. But once he got there, he was too busy to think about anything other than what he needed to do.

Dale called for a couple of ambulances to deal with the brave ones who hurt themselves in their panic to escape. All their names and other information were taken before they were hauled away. Two of the deputies involved in the raid followed the ambulances to the hospital to ensure that no one tried to escape.

Mack assisted with the questioning and gathering of informa-tion, then hauled three of the adult males in the group to jail. After everyone who was captured was safely locked away, he assisted Dale in calling the parents of the prisoners under eighteen.

When all that was completed, Dale told him, "Okay, Mack, you've put in a long enough day. Why don't you take poor, very patient Linda home now? You both look exhausted."

"Are you sure you don't want me to help with the parents?"

"I am very sure I don't want you to help deal with the parents tonight. I know how you feel about all this, and I not only don't blame you, I agree with you. But we don't need any serious confrontations right now. And as tired as I know you are, I doubt that you will have much patience with them. So get out of here. Get some sleep and don't worry about what time you get out on the job tomorrow. We'll manage."

Mack did as Dale requested without argument, as much for Linda's sake as because he knew Dale was right. He wouldn't have any patience with parents of the kind of kids that were in the gang.

When he and Linda got to her home, he was sure they would each go to their own bed and quickly fall asleep. Instead, they had a glass of wine as they relaxed on the couch.

"I know that we're both pretty tired, Mack," Linda said, "but I want to talk to you about what has happened, what is happening, between us."

"I'm sorry if it's bothering you," Mack said, surprised at how serious she sounded. "I would hate it if I've hurt you in any way."

"No, no! It's nothing at all like that. For me, what happened went far beyond the physical part. That was as good for me as it could ever get, but what's between you and I, it all goes way beyond sex, friendship, or even love. You saved my life. You got shot doing it. Just a few inches, and that bullet could have killed you. You were forced to kill a man while you were saving me. I know you well enough to know that that isn't something easy for you to live with. That alone is enough to bond us together fairly strong."

"You're not upset with me then?"

"Only in good ways. You've upset me only because you've changed my life, because the way I feel about you will be with me forever. Even in an afterlife, if there is one. I admit that I was attracted to you from the first time I met you. I remember dancing with you at your uncle's party you guys had for him and Wanda. I knew then, I felt it then while we were dancing, that there was something there, some kind of strange connection between you and I. I also very much love my husband, and that and the needs of your life are going to take us back to before yesterday. Before we shared what we've shared. But don't you, and don't you let me, waste a moment of time we have. Even if it's something as simple as just standing close together or holding hands. And I want you to know that this, and I mean all of this, will not hurt Dave. When I told you that we have a special kind of relationship, I meant that we both know that it is impossible for just one person to fill, to satisfy, another person's life. It's also important to be able to share who and what you are with more than one person. So we have lived our life together living by that truth. It has made us closer and, I think, helped us to maintain the same love we shared way back when we were first married. So no matter what happens between you and me, you should never feel guilty about Dave and me."

Mack took a deep breath, as he tried to find the right words to answer her. "I wish I had the words to tell you all the things I'm feeling about this, Linda, but I don't. So I'm just going to say that I agree with everything you've said. And I do remember dancing with you that night. Somehow, because of who you and I are, you made me feel whole again, that no matter what had happened, there was something to hold on to. And every time I remember dancing with you, I smile. Just like I'll always smile when I think of you in the future. I want you to know too, if it was another time, another place, or even another life, I don't think we would, or could, walk away from each other."

"No, Mack," she said, pausing to kiss him, "we couldn't ever do it."

She set her wine glass down, took his hand, and led him to the shower. After the shower, they made love. It was a long, slow, lingering love. And then, as they held each other, sleep came.

CHAPTER 21

THEY WERE IN THE KITCHEN, drinking coffee, both quietly filled with the thoughts of all they shared. Linda, who held her head down with her eyes closed, suddenly lifted her head. She had tears in her eyes. She stood and took Mack's hand.

"I'm sorry," she said with a catch in her voice, "but this day is not going to start this way or end this way. It has all meant too much."

She led him to her bedroom. It was more than an hour before they dressed again and another half hour before they left the house.

Mack went into the hospital with Linda when they got there. Dave Sanders was finally awake. Linda knew she couldn't give him the hug that she wanted to give him because of his injury, but she did manage to lightly kiss him. He was only able to take her hand and hold it.

Then he looked at Mack. "I've been told by the staff here about what you did for Linda. I want you to know that I will be forever grateful for that. If you ever need anything that I can give you or help you with, please just tell me. I'll give it or do it in a second."

"You don't owe me anything, Dave. I'm just damn glad that I was there when I was. It was the least I could do for two people as good and decent as you two are. But now that I know you're going to be okay and that Linda is in good hands, I need to go. I'm sure that

Dale could use my help right now. And, Linda, call me when you're ready to leave, and I'll take you home. Von Herter is still a menace."

"I will, Mack. I will call you."

Mack couldn't help but wonder, as he drove to the police station, about his feeling for Linda. She had definitely filled a large place in his heart. A place that would always be just for her. Yet he was genuinely happy that Dave Sanders was now on his road to recovery. He also knew, just from the look on Linda's face when she realized that Dave was awake, that he and Linda had returned to the place they lived before Dave was shot. But even though it left him with a somewhat empty feeling inside, he was happy for those two fine people.

When he got to the station, Dale asked him to go out to the refuge to help Rich Hayden, and the deputy who was already out there get the snowmobiles that were involved in the previous night's activity organized so they could be hauled away. All of them were being confiscated, regardless of who the owner was. That included the machine the mayor's son was driving. This time, no one from the sheriff's office or the staff that ran the refuge cared even a little bit if someone like the mayor of Kingsburg thought they were above the law. All of their threats fell on deaf ears.

Mack spent the rest of his day gathering together and loading snowmobiles at the refuge. There was still some day left when they finished, but Mack gave up and went home. Roy and Wanda were getting ready to leave when he got there.

"Where are you going?" Mack asked.

"We thought," Roy said, giving Mack a broad smile, "that we'd give your dad and his guest a little time alone. We're going to walk the new farm for a while, check out the boundaries, and such. We've got a third pair of snowshoes in back. We've got them with us, just in case you happened along."

"The guest wouldn't be Theresa would it."

"It would, so be nice and come with us."

"Sure, as long as you two fill me in on what all has been going on."

"There isn't much to tell, Mack. She stayed here after the raid at the refuge. She slept in your bed, not Ben's. They both slept late and have spent the day drinking coffee and getting better acquainted. But it was beginning to seem a bit crowded with me and Wanda there."

"Do you mean, Roy, you think it's getting serious?"

"That's hard to tell. It seems though, that if it is, it wouldn't be a bad thing for either one of them. It's a sure bet that she needs something to hang on to, and it's damn sure Ben's been alone way too long."

Mack smiled. "I have to say, I was hoping they'd at least become friends. If it's more, I couldn't be happier for them."

"Neither could we," Wanda said. "Neither could we."

The three of them stayed until dark, exploring the new farm and planning where to put new fences and buildings. They would have stayed longer, but Linda called for her ride home, and it was too dark to see anyway.

"So," Roy said, "you're still watching out for her."

"I will be for at least the next few days. Von Herter's lawyer got him out of jail, and he's still a dangerous man."

"He is," Roy agreed, "so you be damned careful."

"I will. I'd much rather shoot one of them than have one of them shoot me."

CHAPTER 22

ERIC VON HERTER WAS EXTREMELY upset with the world where Mack Thomas lived. He wanted revenge, and he wanted it bad. And simply killing Mack, which he fully intended to have done, wasn't enough. He wanted to do more to hurt as many people who were Mack's friends as he possibly could. One of the main people currently on his list was Lisa Anderson. He considered her to be someone who thought she was much bigger and better than she was. So before he had her killed too, he fully intended to stop her New Year's Eve protest.

To his way of thinking, no one, especially just a kid, should be allowed to disrupt or in any way interfere with something as great as the resort, Heritage Preservation Minnesota. Besides, he owned stock in the company and was part owner of two of the construction companies that had done work related to the resort. One of the companies built the river dam that created the lake and the other built the bridge where the protest was going to be held.

It was his plan to stop the protest by filling the bridge with heavy equipment. Before the protest started, he would have his own employees fill the bridge with bulldozers, backhoes, loaders, and other equipment, so there was no room for anyone to stand on the bridge and protest. And if anyone tried to get on the bridge anyway, he would have his men remove them.

He would wait until the protest thing had been defeated before he went after Lisa Anderson and the two girls helping her. Linda and Dave Sanders, he would get when he found it convenient. Mack, he wanted to have taken out as soon as possible. There were many others on his list of enemies, but most of them would have to wait. It was possible, after all, that someone in law enforcement might get suspicious if he had too many killed at the same time.

CHAPTER 23

DAVE SANDERS WAS ASLEEP WHEN Mack got to his room to pick up Linda. She was sitting in a chair near the bed, and she smiled at Mack when she saw him. She stood up, kissed Dave on the cheek, and then hugged Mack.

"I'm really tired," she said, "so let's go. I told Dave that we would be going when you got here, even if he was sleeping. After I told him about all of the adventures I've had since all this started, he agreed that it would be a good idea to get home at a decent hour and get a good night's sleep."

"Were you and I one of the adventures you told him about?" Mack asked.

"Not directly. I think he knows and understands why, that there's more to our relationship than a simple friendship, but he isn't at all upset by it. He's mostly just grateful for what you did and for what you're still doing. Maybe someday, he and I will talk more about it, but for now, it's not a cause for concern."

"Good. It would bother me if anything I did slowed or hurt his recovery."

"Don't worry, Mack. It won't."

"Now that I feel better about that, I'm curious. And I do mean that I'm not upset, only curious, about us. I definitely got the feeling this morning when we found Dave awake that our relationship had pretty much moved back to where it was when all this started."

"We can never move it back to that, Mack. The way I feel about you, and the way you feel about me, that love can never go back. But for right now, like maybe today and tomorrow, and maybe even next week and beyond, we'll just be the best friends we could be. As for the rest, let's just let time play it all out. Because for whatever time brings, we will always have these past few days inside us, just as we will always have the feelings inside us. If for any reason, sometime in the future, it leads us back to those few days, we'll deal with it then."

Her words left Mack with mixed feelings, but he knew she was right about everything she said. On one side, he felt a letdown, yet on the other side, he knew it was for the best. No matter what, the best choice for them, and for everyone else in their lives, was for them to get on with living, the same as they'd always done.

It wasn't until they got to Linda's that she wondered about Theresa. And that was because she wasn't there.

"Where's Theresa, Mack? She should have been home last night. Was she? I never thought to check on her. I hope she's not in any kind of trouble."

"I'm sorry," Mack said, trying not to laugh but failing. "Theresa's just fine. She's with the safest person I know. She's at my father's."

"She's still with Ben? Now that's a surprise. Not that Theresa would stay there, but that your father would have her."

"I guess it would be. To you and to most people. Not to me though. Dad' had some kind of feelings for her since they first met. I know, he didn't approve of all the mistakes she made and it sometimes showed. Even so, he always knew that she was a good person, that she really deserved better than what she got. And for me, if they've got something going, I couldn't be happier. For both of them."

"Even after all the things she did?"

"Linda, what did she do that was so terrible? Having been a teenage boy, I can tell you that it wasn't much. Likely as not, it was a long way from terrible for any of them. So yes, even after all the things she did, I still approve of it if there's something going on between her and my dad."

Linda shook her head, then looked into his eyes.

"Damn it," she said, "you sure are one hell of a man. I want you to shut up for a while though. Or else…"

CHAPTER 24

LISA, TERRY, AND JO WERE making the final plans for the protest march at the refuge on New Year's Eve. They were making some progress, but Lisa was concerned about Terry. She was unusually quiet, seemingly subdued in her speech and nearly everything else she did.

Finally, Lisa had to ask, "What is the matter, Terry? You just aren't yourself today."

"Oh, I'm okay. I've just been thinking about all the kids arrested at the refuge. I just wonder what's going to happen to them. I know that what they did was terrible, but I hope they're not in too much trouble."

"I don't agree with you about that," Jo said. "Most of them are the kids who think they're better than the rest of us. They were out there killing deer and doing it in a terribly cruel way. It was much worse than just shooting them. So as far as I'm concerned, if they all go to jail, I won't care."

"I know all that, Jo. I guess I just wish we could all try to get along better. We just seem to be always finding ways to hurt each other. Like those three men who were murdered. I bet that what they were doing when they were murdered was trying to hurt someone. Why aren't men like that in jail?"

"Some of them are," Lisa said. "And some of them that hurt us are dead."

"True," Terry smiled, "and maybe some of them who are still alive and not in jail have learned enough so no one will have to kill them too."

"Maybe," Lisa told her, "if, and I mean if, any men like that are smart enough to learn anything. But let's not talk about them any longer. We still have some things to finish planning if we're going to make the protest work the way we want it to. Even if we can't do anything to stop all the abusive men in the world, maybe the protest will help save the refuge that's left and keep that horrible resort from taking any more of it."

"You're right, Lisa," Terry said. "I don't think it'll do any good to kill any more of those horrible men anyway. It seems like that even if one of those creeps die, there's always another to take his place. So you're right, Lisa, the refuge is more important than killing more of those men."

Lisa didn't say anything more about the men who were killed, but she did find the way Terry phrased her last sentence a bit strange.

CHAPTER 25

MACK STAYED WITH LINDA TWO more nights. They were both very quiet, and the conversations in the evenings were on subjects that weren't too personal. Linda and Mack tried not to talk about their own relationship, and neither one of them asked Theresa, when she was there in the evening, about what she was doing.

Dave Sanders was released from the hospital the day after that, and everyone involved agreed that Linda should be safe at home. They arranged it so that Mack, or any deputy available at the time, would escort her if she needed to go anywhere.

While that was going on, Theresa started working with Ben part time in the greenhouse. Detective Paul Danielson's wife had also spent some time in the greenhouse. Much to everyone's surprise, they became instant friends. The fact that Teresa had been married to a cop, even if he was a corrupt one, and Paul's wife, Mary, still was, gave them a lot in common to talk about. And the more they talked and the better they knew each other, the closer they became.

So with everything quieter, Mack returned to the life he had before Dave and Linda were attacked. The first night he was free, he drove to the Anderson farm to see Beth. The hug and kiss she gave him told him that she was glad to see him.

They went out that night, and after a good meal and a cold beer, Mack took a drive out into one of the few secluded spots left in the refuge. They made love there, in the front seat of Mack's truck. It was crowded but satisfying anyway.

After, Beth told him, "That was a long time coming, Mack. I was beginning to wonder if it was ever going to happen again."

"I know. It's just that sometimes, life gets in the way of the things we want. And when you're a cop, the sometimes seem to get to be more often."

"I understand that, Mack. But I also realize that they'll happen more often with you than anybody else, given who you are. I'm not complaining, but I don't want you to ever forget that when those things happen, I'll always be home waiting for you."

"I won't," he said, hoping that the guilt he felt hearing her words didn't show in his voice.

"I know you won't. You're too good a man to ever let me down that way."

Because of Beth's very early morning schedule to help with the milking on the dairy farm, they left the refuge then.

When they got back to the farm, Lisa came outside. She hurried to the truck and waited for Mack to get out.

"I need to talk to you about something, Mack. It's something that I don't know how to deal with."

"Do you want me to leave you alone to talk to Mack?" Beth asked her.

"No, I want you to stay. You might be able to help me too."

"Okay," Mack said, "tell me the problem and I'll do the best I can to help."

"It's Terry. She's been acting kind of strange lately, and today she said something that scared me. We were talking about those men who were murdered, and when I asked that we talk about the protest march because the refuge is more important, she said, 'You're right, the refuge is more important than killing more of those men.' It wasn't just what she said that bothers me, Mack, it was the way she said it."

"Why, exactly, did it bother you?"

"Because it almost sounded like she killed them. If it's something like that, she needs our help, doesn't she?"

"After all that she's been through, yes, she does need our help. No matter what, she could very well need our help anyway. I promise that tomorrow, I'll talk to Dale about how we can go about getting her some help."

"Okay, Mack, I knew I could count on you."

Mack was fairly sure then that Terry was the one guilty of the murders. At the same time, he had no doubts at all that she didn't belong in prison. She'd been hurt enough for anyone's lifetime.

He kissed them both goodnight, Lisa on the forehead and gave Beth a light peck on the lips.

As Mack left the farm, his head was so full of all the things happening around him, that he failed to notice that the headlights that started to follow him soon after he left the farm, then stayed with him on every turn on the way home. When he did notice, he knew it could easily be a coincidence, while at the same time he knew from recent past experience that it could be something serious. He also knew that the people who worked for Von Herter were too stupid to be able to be even slightly subtle when they tailed someone.

So to be sure, Mack detoured over to the refuge, then at the bridge left the road and drove down to the lake. The idiots behind him followed him down and out onto the lake. The man in the passenger side of the pickup behind him fired two quick shots. One went wide and the other hit the tailgate of Mack's truck. Mack knew he had them at that point. Using the superior power and speed of his pickup, he did a series of maneuvers that quickly put him behind them.

He took his pistol out of its shoulder holster, then drove along the right side of the truck. First, he shot out the right rear tire, then moved up and took out the front tire. The driver of that truck nearly lost it then and was barely able to keep it from rolling over before he managed to bring it to a stop.

Mack was instantly out of his truck, his gun in his hand, and was able to open the passenger side door open before the man riding there had a chance to do anything. Mack pulled him out and he landed face first in the snow. Mack then reached inside the truck and fired once through the windshield. The driver of the truck dropped his weapon.

"Out, now," Mack told him. "And move slow."

Mack thought about arresting the two men, but then noticed that they were on the far end of the lake from the road and got a better idea. He knew that a lawyer would get them out in a day or two, so he decided that he would deal out a far better punishment.

"I hope this has been fun for you two so far because it won't be quite as much fun from now on."

"You can't do nothin' to us here. This is the refuge. Cops ain't got no authority here."

"Well, you're wrong about that. But it doesn't matter a damn to me anyway. For now, I want you both to take off your boots and put them in the back of my truck."

"Why do you want us to do that?"

"You'll see. Just do it. Throw your gloves in there too." They did what they were told to do. "Now pop the hood on your truck and pull out all the spark plug wires." They did it. "Now back off a ways." They moved back a few feet. Mack picked their guns out of the snow and threw them into the back of his truck. "Now give me your cell phones." Mack put them in on seat of his truck.

"What are ya goin' ta do ta us?" the driver of the truck whined.

"Absolutely nothing," Mack explained. "It's been a long day and I'm tired, so I'm going to let you both go."

"But what are we supposed to do? You got our boots, so we can't walk out of here. We'll freeze."

"Maybe, maybe not. I certainly don't care either way."

"You better know, Thomas, Von Herter ain't gonna like this. You're a dead man for sure this time."

Mack laughed as he got back in his truck. "That might be possible. But if I were you, I'd find another line of work because next time we cross paths, I fully intend on killing the both of you. I'll leave the cell phones somewhere between here and the road. If you can find them in the snow, you'll be able to call someone for a ride."

He stopped about halfway to the road, then threw the cell phones belonging to the two men as far as he could. Each in a different direction.

CHAPTER 26

MACK GOT A BIG SURPRISE when he got home. Theresa was there and sitting on Ben's lap. Wanda and Roy were sitting on the couch across from them, and all four of them acted as if a woman sitting on Ben's lap was perfectly normal. Never mind, it was something no one had seen for years. Not since Mack's mother died.

Mack did his best to act as though it wasn't at all surprising to see her in his lap. But it did leave him momentarily speechless.

Ben spoke first. "I know, Mack. This is a surprise for you. It's a surprise for me too. I never thought I'd ever have this happen to me again, but it has. I hope you approve."

"I more than approve, Dad, I couldn't be happier for you."

"I told him," Roy said, "you would react that way."

"No other way to react."

"Now that we settled that," Wanda said. "What all have you been up to lately?"

"Not much. I finally got a chance to spend some time with Beth tonight. Then I had a little run-in with a couple of Von Herter's men on the way home."

Mack's last comment caught Roy's attention. He knew Mack well enough to know that what he called a little run-in could be a whole lot more.

"So what was your *little* run-in about?"

Mack filled them in on the episode with the two men.

"You mean that you really left them out in the refuge like that?" Ben asked.

"I did."

"Weren't you at all worried about them freezing?"

"No. They might get some frostbite. The might even lose a toe or two. But if they do, it's only because they deserve it."

"That's true. It should tell Von Herter something too. Not that he's smart enough to listen."

"He isn't," Mack said. "Given the things he's been doing lately, I think he'd pretty much lost it. He's probably crazy enough now to do just about anything. But as bad as that is, he's going to make a big mistake soon, and it's going to be one that's big enough for me to hang him with."

"I sure do hope so," Ben said. "There isn't much I'd rather see more than Von Herter locked up in jail permanently."

They talked about Von Herter for a few more minutes, then Roy told Mack some good news. "Emmett and Emma have moved out. Tomorrow, Wanda and I are going to move in. It'll be nice for Ben and Teresa to have some privacy too."

"You know," Ben argued, "you and Wanda are welcome to stay here as long as you want. Permanent is just fine too."

"I know that, Ben. But I've been where you are now, and it'll be better if Wanda and I move over to the new place. Give it another year or so, and it won't matter so much."

"Roy's right," Mack agreed, then turned toward Roy. "And talking about the new place, I've been so busy I haven't had the chance to check it out or even pay any attention to it, so I don't know how anything is coming along. Specifically, the new guest house. Have they delivered the manufactured home yet?"

"It came yesterday and the manager of the sales lot where you bought it said that it'll be set up and ready to go before Christmas. A lot of the work is done, given all the rubble from the burned house has been cleaned up. And the guy who's going to set up the new house said it will be fairly easy to hook up to the existing well and sewage system."

"That's good news," Mack said. "Christmas isn't that far away. And when it's done, I think I'll move into it," he looked at Ben and smiled, "so I can give them some privacy too."

"I think that's enough about us needing privacy," Ben argued. "There's nothing going on that gives us the need for so much privacy."

"Ben," Wanda told him, "you need it just to get to know each other. We all know that. And even if you don't need us to be gone for a while, Theresa does. Given time, there won't be so much, if any, need. But believe me, Ben, there is now."

Theresa didn't say anything in response to Wanda's words. She just had a big smile on her face well before Wanda stopped talking.

Mack went to bed a short time later without anyone mentioning anything about sleeping arrangements. For him, Ben's private life was just that. *His* private life.

CHAPTER 27

MACK WOKE UP IN A cold sweat. The dream had been vivid, and he knew it would be a while before he slept again. So he got up, went to the kitchen, and poured himself a cold glass of water from the water filter on the refrigerator door. When he went into the living room, Roy and Wanda joined him. She looked as bad as Mack felt.

As soon as they saw each other, Mack and Wanda knew what had happened. Their dreams, their nightmares, were the same.

"It wasn't the past, was it, Mack?"

"No," Mack agreed, "it wasn't, Wanda. This one was new. There was water, but a lot of ice and a lot of people screaming. Someone saying something about swimming. I could see pictures of things happening, but I couldn't tell where it was."

"That's the way my dreams were too. I saw a lot that was new, things that are going to happen, I just couldn't tell where. I heard the screams and the voice about swimming too."

"You know," Roy said, "that you guys scare the shit out of the rest of us when you have the same dreams."

"It scares the shit out of us too," Wanda said.

"That's an understatement," Mack told them. "And it's a fact, whatever it is coming, it's going to be bad. I sure wish to hell one of us could figure it out."

Before anyone could say anything else, Ben and Teresa joined them. They were both wearing bathrobes, but it was obvious that was all they were wearing. In spite of everything, no matter how much his dreams were worrying him, Mack couldn't totally hide his smile when he saw them. It had been such a very long time, but now it appeared Ben had finally found someone to share his life with. The kind of sharing that can't be done with anyone but the right woman.

"So," Ben asked, "what's all the commotion about?"

Mack and Wanda told him about their dreams.

"This is weird," Theresa said, "you guys having the same dreams that way. How long have you been doing this?"

"It's hard to say exactly," Wanda explained. "We started having similar dreams while we were in Texas, and they've been getting more alike since then. We don't know why."

"At least this time," Ben said, "you're in the same place. It seems that they bother both of you more when you're in different places. So if you're going to be okay, I think I'm going back to bed."

"We're okay, Dad," Mack said.

"We'll be fine," Wanda agreed.

Ben went back to bed and Theresa went with him.

Roy chuckled when they were gone. "Who would have thought, not that damn long ago, that Ben would be where he so obviously is now?"

"None of us," Mack said. "But it is definitely a good thing to see."

They all went back to bed then. Mack had trouble falling asleep, and when he finally did, he slept past his normal getting up time in the morning.

So when he met with Dale and Paul for coffee at Katie's Kafe in the morning, they were already there.

"Sorry I'm late," he told them. "I had a real bad night and I overslept a little. Wanda and I had the same dreams, and they weren't good ones."

"Something new?" Dale asked.

"Mostly new. A lot of ice this time, with people screaming, but with water too, and someone talking about swimming." He went on to tell them more about the dreams.

"Do you really think," Paul asked, "that those dreams are going to actually happen? Or are they just bad dreams?"

"When we have them, we always hope they are just bad dreams. The trouble is, they pretty much always come true. Maybe not exactly the same as the dreams, but with the same result."

"Do you know where all this is going to happen?"

"No, no idea at all. I'm just going to have to be careful and be ready when something does happen."

"I think," Dale said, "we'll all have to be careful and be ready for some kind of disaster."

"Speaking of disasters," Paul said, "at least there haven't been any new murders."

"Maybe we'll get lucky," Mack said, "and there won't be any more."

"Do you think though, that if Terry is in fact the one who committed them, she'll be able to stop?"

"I don't have any idea whether she could or not, Paul. I'm just hoping that because she's really a good person, that it is possible."

"I think it's possible," Dale said. "I know that the trauma she went through was a horror story, but I still believe she is capable enough to overcome it and stop. I hope so anyway, because even if she did kill those men, I don't think she should go to prison."

"I completely agree with that," Mack said.

"And speaking of prison," Dale said, "why didn't you arrest those two characters you had the run-in with last night? Both of them are in the hospital with some badly frostbitten feet."

"That's simple," Mack explained. "I keep getting told that I'm too violent, too hard on people who try to kill me. So I decided to be really nice last night, after they shot at me, with the intent to kill me, and let them go. I didn't even scold them for their bad behavior."

"But you took their boots and gloves. Did you really think they could walk out of there without a problem?"

"I didn't see any big reason why they couldn't. They still had socks on to cover their feet, and they had pockets in their jackets to put their hands in. So how could there have been a problem. I was just trying to make sure that they couldn't chase me fast enough to catch me and kill me."

Dale couldn't argue the point with Mack any longer. He and Paul were laughing too hard to be able to say anything, let alone argue.

When Dale could finally talk again, he told Mack, "When Von Herter called me this morning to complain about the way you treated his employees, I told him what part of his body he could stuff his complaints."

"Good," Mack said. "That makes us one small step closer to the day Von Herter gets his."

After a little more discussion about everything going on, they left Katie's. Mack wasn't sure what to do with the day, and he gradually drifted into the refuge. He decided to stop at the headquarters and talk to the manager, Rich Hayden, so see if there had been any recent poaching.

When he walked in, there was a loud argument going on in Rich's office. He asked the woman at the reception desk about it.

"It's just another parent angry about his kid being arrested after the raid the other night."

"Has Rich been getting a lot of this kind of thing?" Mack asked.

"Just enough to be very aggravating. This guy's worse though. He claims to be someone real important with the bank. I could hear him threaten Rich about his account there."

"Really? Well, I don't think Rich deserves that, so I think I'll stick my nose into their conversation. After all, I'm the one who was behind that raid."

Mack went into Rich's office without knocking. The man yelling at Rich turned to Mack and pointed at the door.

"Get the fuck out of here," he ordered, "this doesn't concern you."

"I think it does," Mack said, keeping his voice at a normal level. "You're jumping the wrong man with your problem. I'm the one you should be screaming at."

"You! Shit! You're nothing! That badge you're wearing doesn't mean shit. You got no authority here. Now get the hell out of here before I knock you on your ass."

Mack laughed. "Is that a threat?"

"You goddamn right it is." He tried to poke his finger into Mack's chest, but Mack grabbed it and twisted it to the edge of breaking. The man groaned loud enough to be heard outside of Rich's office.

"You don't want to be doing things like that to me." Mack let his finger go. "And now, I think it's time for you to leave. These people here don't need nor do they deserve your childish behavior."

"Goddamn you. I'll show you a thing or two." He took a swing at Mack.

Mack could sense it coming and had no trouble ducking under it. He simply pushed the man away. Rich grabbed him then and told him that it was time to leave.

But the man wasn't ready to give it up, and this time, he tried to hit Rich. The blow just grazed the side of Rich's head but did no damage. It was enough for Rich though, and he decked the man. Mack cuffed him while he was down.

"Just what the hell do you think you're doing?" the man screamed. "You can't do this to me. I'll have both your asses before the day is over. And you can bet that your accounts at the bank are toast too. I run that bank now, and you've had it in this county."

Mack laughed. "What bank is it that a common criminal like you runs?"

"I run the Kingsburg Bank. In a short time, I'm going to be president of that bank. So I can do anything I please to your accounts."

"Harley Anderson is president of the bank, so your lies are going to get you nowhere with us."

"Harley is going to retire soon, then I'll be taking over. You'll both see what you'll get then."

Mack couldn't help laughing again. "I suppose I will, but in the meantime, you better get a lawyer. You are under arrest." Mack read him his rights.

"Just a minute now," the man whined, "I didn't do anything that you can arrest me for."

"The fact is," Mack explained, "you did. You committed two counts of assault. I have every intention of filing charges against you. I'm sure Rich will be doing the same. Then I'll be giving Harley a call, and I'm going to request that he give Twilabee a call to let him know why you're in jail. Given the fact that Twilabee is CEO of your bank's parent corporation, he might have some opinions about your behavior. He might even listen to my suggestion that he fire your sorry ass."

"Wait a minute now. You don't have to carry things to that extreme. I was just upset about what happened to my boy."

"I'm not," Mack told him. "I'm not one damn bit upset about your boy. He was involved in some of the nastiest, dirtiest criminal activity there is. I very much hope that the kind of cruelty he was involved in ends up giving him some type of grief for the rest of his life."

"How can you say that? All they did is kill some stupid, useless deer."

"Useless? I don't think so." Mack was angry now, but doing a good job of controlling it. "Those deer serve a far greater purpose than you, your nasty brat, and all the members of that gang combined will ever serve. So yes, you are going to jail, and you will stay there until your lawyer gets you out."

"Everything he said," Rich added, "goes for me too."

The man was very subdued on the way back to the office. Mack was tempted to put the man in the back of his truck for the ride, but given his typical banker's condition, he was afraid he might not make it.

After all the papers were filed and Mack had a second conversation with Harley Anderson, Mack stopped by the criminal banker's jail cell.

"Harley is really upset with you," Mack told him.

"Why should Harley care about any of this?"

"Mostly, I guess, because you postponed his retirement."

"How did I do that?"

"By earning a transfer. It seems that a small town in Alabama needs a head teller. So that's where Twilabee is sending you."

"Oh my god! You did all that to me? Just for this?"

"No," Mack said, "you did it to yourself."

CHAPTER 28

HE WAS A LOT MORE confident when he rode alone now, after making many trips through the refuge. He would never get lost now. On every ride, he made sure to drive past the shack where he cut the lock. So far, no one had discovered that he had broken in and removed all of the things that he had.

That meant that no one would be suspecting his plan. A plan that was getting better all the time. He had gone online and Googled all the information he needed. He knew too, that he had everything he needed to make it work.

He felt good about himself now, and every time he rode by his target, his confidence grew. It also excited him as the time drew nearer. Soon, on nights dark enough so he wouldn't be seen, he would be making preparations.

What he had planned was going to shake up everyone, and when he told some of his friends that he did it, he was sure it would impress them. He especially wanted to impress the new girl, Terry. He really liked her, even if she did ride, at least once, with one of the older men who were part of the now dead Deer Runners club.

And when he thought about how much he hated them, it made him feel good that what he was going to do was so much bigger and more exciting than chasing deer ever was.

This night, it was fairly dark, so he stopped by his target and walked over part of it, checking out the spots he thought would be best to make his plan work.

He felt very satisfied with himself when he completed his walk and then headed home on his snowmobile.

CHAPTER 29

A FTER THE INCIDENT WITH THE would-be bank president, things quieted down a lot. Even with all the problems Clayborne County was facing, the Christmas holiday time always seemed to calm things a bit. There were a lot of things about the holiday that Mack didn't believe in or like much, but he did appreciate the fact that for him and his family, along with most families he knew, that's what Christmas was really about. Family. And time together as a family.

For Mack, this year was going to be the most special Christmas he could remember since his mother died. Because this year was going to be the first time since then that he was going to spend it with both Ben and Roy. That was just the beginning though. Of course, Wanda would be there. They wouldn't have any kind of a celebration without her. The thing that was almost as great as having all his family around, it was the fact that they were going to have a lot more than that.

Wanda and Theresa had gotten together and organized a special celebration for Christmas Eve. First, because Theresa and Linda were sisters and because Dave was still not fully recovered, they were invited. Their daughter, Kathy, was invited too, along with her fiancé, Sheriff Dale Magee. Paul Danielson and his wife Mary were new to the area, and because they hadn't made any plans and had become such good friends, they were coming. Beth had made her normal

156

plans with her family, but when Wanda told her about the Christmas Eve they were going to have, she knew she had to be there too, even though she wouldn't be there until after the milking was done. She could spend Christmas Day with her family. The Anderson family was invited too, but they already had plans to spend the evening with Bob Anderson's brother and his family down in Minneapolis.

Ben, Wanda, and Theresa spent the afternoon preparing the dinner. They made two kinds of meatballs. One kind was Swedish, with allspice, clove, and lots of nutmeg. The other kind was Ben's special recipe that started with two parts ground round to one part top quality ground pork sausage and finished with Ben's secret spices. They also cooked several rings of Swedish potato sausage.

The side dishes were mashed potatoes loaded with butter and a rich brown gravy on the side. Baked butternut squash, also served with plenty of butter, and for those who liked it that way, plenty of brown gravy. Corn, put up fresh during the growing season, rounded out the main meal.

For dessert, they had apple pie made from fresh apples and pumpkin pie. This time, the pumpkin came out of a can.

Because the kitchen was bigger, it had a formal dining room, and the living room had more and better seating, they had the dinner at the farm house that Roy and Wanda had just moved into.

It turned out to be an excellent choice. It had the feel of an old-time farm house, which was warm and homey. Yet it still had a modern kitchen, central heating, and even two bathrooms. The house, and the fact that everyone one there was one way or another very fond of each other, made the evening move along as pleasantly as a gathering like that possibly could.

Only one thing was slightly out of balance. Although they did their best to hide it, whenever Mack's and Linda's eyes met, they told stories to anyone who noticed their reaction to each other.

Fortunately, only three people did. Dave did but totally ignored it. He knew and understood completely what it was about. Wanda noticed, and it made her wonder what it was all about. Because of the already close relationship she had with Mack, she somehow sensed that whatever the connection he and Linda had was okay, but she was also sure that there was something very special between them. She decided that she would remain silent about it with everyone, including Roy, at least until she got the chance to ask Mack about it.

Beth was the third person to notice them. She did right away and continued to watch them during the early part of the meal. The feelings she got from watching them, though, ended up something way different from what she expected when she first noticed what was happening. She was sure that there was something serious between them but wasn't exactly sure what, other than love, that it was. In the end, she had a very strong feeling that it was the kind of thing that went beyond what she could right now understand, but that whatever it was, it was no threat to her or her relationship with Mack.

One person, though, stood out during the meal. Theresa seemed to literally glow. From the tone of her voice, the small things she said, the way she moved, and most of all, her constant smile, her happiness was obviously complete.

Ben and Roy were also obviously enjoying themselves. They carried on the way they usually did, but all the kidding, arguing, and teasing was gently done. So gently done, that it was hard sometimes to tell that they were doing it.

Dale and Kathy were always part of the conversation going on and were obviously happy to be with all the people there. And it was equally obvious that Dave and Linda were very proud of their daughter and the man she was with. And like everyone else there, they were very much a part of the group.

Paul and Mary were made to feel so much at home, to know that they were part of this group, that there was no doubt in their minds that they made the right moves when they made Clayborne County their home.

After the delicious meal, which left everyone over-full, all the females told the men to relax while they did the cleanup. Only Mack was foolish enough to protest, insisting that he should help, that it wasn't fair that they should do all the hard work. Roy was the one who managed to convince him to forget about it. He knew that doing the cleanup together is something they wanted to do, and even more, it gave them a chance to talk without any men around.

After the cleanup was completed, Kathy led everyone, with her near-perfect, crystal-clear voice, as they sang Christmas carols. Everyone sang along as best they could. Everyone except Mack. The music somehow brought back all the memories of the people now forever gone from his life. So he quietly moved behind the group and silently listened. But someone noticed, and soon Wanda was standing next to him, holding his hand. She got him through it.

Linda watched them, wishing that it was her hand that Mack was holding.

It was after midnight before anyone was willing to let the night go. When they did, they all left about the same time. Mack and Beth had, with the exception of Wanda and Roy who lived there, the shortest trip home. They spent the rest of the night in the new, now finished and furnished guest house. Mack was happy that he had decided to buy a manufactured home to replace the old guest house. Any other type of construction, and the house wouldn't be ready yet.

Having it ready now meant he would have the rest of the night with Beth. A time together they both needed.

After they made love that night, Beth said, "I know there's something with you and Linda. I know it's okay, but some other time when you're ready, I'd like it if you'd tell me about it."

"I will tell you, as long as you will wait until that other time."

"That's all I ask."

With Mack holding Beth close, sleep came easy for them then.

CHAPTER 30

THE NEXT WEEK WENT BY fast, with Lisa and her STR group getting ready for the big protest march, and Mack and Dale planning the best way to handle the now expected large crowd.

They were lucky with the fact that there were no more murders or other major crimes. As always, during the holiday season, there were more than the average number of DUIs and drunk and disorderly arrests, but it was otherwise quiet.

There were a lot of rumors floating around about Von Herter stopping the protest, but no one was sure how he was going to manage it. Only he knew what he had planned, and he wasn't going to tell anyone until the day of the protest what those plans were.

Many of the men who worked for him might have figured it out, but since they either didn't care about what he was doing or they were too stupid to add two and two, they didn't figure it out. Even when he had them start moving heavy equipment on to the county road near the bridge the day before the protest, most of them weren't sure what he was up to.

When New Year's Eve day arrived, the weather was clear and mild. Mild for Minnesota meant in the midtwenties. If it had been what most people who lived in Minnesota called cold, it would have been in the minus twenties.

Everyone involved in the protest was happy about the weather. It meant that the odds for a large turnout was very likely.

Von Herter was happy with the weather too. It meant that the men he had working later in the afternoon than usual for New Year's Eve day, at least wouldn't have the weather to bitch about along with their other complaints. And they would be working later because Von Herter didn't have them start to move the equipment on to the bridge until two hours before the protest was due to arrive at the bridge.

When he first started moving the machines onto the bridge, he kept them in one lane so traffic could still move across it. It wasn't until a very short while before the protesters arrived that he moved the rest of the equipment to block both lanes. It was then that he told his men what he had planned.

A few of his men complained, but most of them were delighted. They thought it would be fun if anyone tried to get on the bridge. If Von Herter didn't want them there, they would enjoy cracking some heads. It wouldn't bother them either, if some of the heads were female. Cracking one head was the same as the other. Just plain fun.

While Von Herter and his men were looking forward to their fun, someone else was finishing up with his own planned fun. Skip Halbertson was completing the wiring connected to several catches of dynamite he had carefully placed on the dam that held back the St. Catherine River. It was basically an earthen dam, and because the company that built it wanted to maximize its profits, it was built to absolute minimum standards.

The management of that company was sure, at the time it was built, that there would never be any natural disaster that could break the damn. After all, Minnesota didn't really have any earthquakes. So what else could do it?

It was too bad they didn't know about teenage boys, hoping to impress girls with their power. And Skip was sure that he had a lot of power now.

How could the girl, Terry, not be impressed? When the dam was gone because he blew it up, and by blowing it up, he would be doing more damage to the resort so many people now hated than any protests. No matter how many there were.

Skip sat back and waited when he finished up and everything was ready. He frequently checked his watch as he waited. He knew the schedule for the protest and planned to wait until he was sure that at least most of the people involved were already on the bridge.

The only thing he was sorry about was the fact that he wouldn't be on that bridge to see all the faces of the people there when they heard the explosion, then watched the water disappear from the lake. That, he knew, would be a fun thing to watch.

And it might have been a fun thing to watch, if it all had gone as he expected it to. It wasn't going to happen the way he hoped and planned though. Von Herter was making sure of that.

His men were now moving the heavy equipment into the other lane. To ensure that it would be extremely difficult for anyone to get very far on the bridge, the first thing anyone trying to use it would encounter were three bulldozers side by side, with their blades lowered. They were set back, about twenty feet from the edge of the bridge where it met the road.

The rest of the considerable numbers of equipment were staggered in various ways to make any movement on the bridge a definite problem. With that part of their job finished, he proudly looked around at what they had done. He knew then that the protest was not going to work out the way all those idiots behind it had planned.

What he did not know, or at least take into consideration, was the fact that with all the equipment now on the bridge, he was over the weight limit of any bridge with the type of construction used on this bridge. Added to that was the fact that all of the steel framework on the upper half of the bridge, which was normally there to strengthen the bridge, was useless on this one. Because of its weight, it actually weakened the bridge.

Something else that he knew about at the time but had forgotten was that all of the concrete used on the bridge, from the footings on up, was of a lower than normal quality. It was winter when the concrete was poured, and because the construction company was in a hurry to get the job done, they used too much chlorine in the concrete. Chlorine caused the concrete to harden faster in cold weather, but if too much is used, it weakens it.

Something he didn't know was that when they were pouring concrete into the footings for the bridge, a serious mistake was made. Originally, the bridge was designed to be just an ordinary river bridge, but that was changed when the management of Land's Magnificent, the company that built the resort changed its concept and name.

It was decided to make the resort appear to be preserving something rather than committing the wholesale destruction of a wildlife refuge that they were guilty of. So they changed its name, and to go along with some other changes, decided to make the new bridge look older and added all the steel framework on top of it.

One of the things they needed to do to make that work was to pour much larger footings. The problem was the foreman on the job ignored the new blueprints when he received them and dug and poured two of the main footings the smaller size needed for the original bridge.

The foreman and the superintendent of the job both knew about the mistake but didn't correct it. They were afraid they might get fired or at least bawled out for the mistake. And being the big strong men that they were, they surely didn't want their bosses mad at them.

Von Herter, however, was a long way from being concerned about anything like that. The only thing he cared about at the moment was stopping the protest. This was his way of proving to everyone that he still had a lot of power in the county and that the sheriff and Mack Thomas and his family couldn't do a damn thing to stop him. No, this time, he was going to show them all that he was nobody to be messed with.

As he gloated about his superiority over all the people in Clayborne County while he paced back and forth in front of his bulldozers, Skip Halbertson was doing much the same thing. The closer it got to the time he planned to set off the dynamite and blow a large hole in the dam, the better he felt about himself. He was finally going to prove to everyone, especially Terry, that he could do really special, really big things.

He was sure, too, that he wouldn't get caught. There was no one around the dam at that time, and as soon as it was blown, he would be on the snowmobile and on his way. Only people that he wanted to know that he did it would ever know about that he was the one who did it. Of that, he was sure. Just as Von Herter was sure that he had developed the perfect plan to screw up the protest.

CHAPTER 31

SINCE IT WAS LISA ANDERSON, Jo Stuart, and Terry Holstrom that started and led the protest movement, it was decided that they would ride in the lead squad car with Dale Magee. So they sat together while they waited for the procession to the refuge bridge to begin. Lisa noticed from the time the three of them got to the high school parking lot where the ride was going to start, that Terry seemed distracted, and what they were doing had lost almost all meaning for her.

So when Jo wandered off and they were alone, Lisa asked her, "What's wrong, Terry? Yesterday you were so excited about today, but now it seems like you don't care about it much."

"I'm sorry. I don't mean to be this way." Terry shook her head as if she was trying to shake away what was in there. "It's just that sometimes I start remembering what all those men did to me, to us, and it really drags me down."

"Maybe you should talk to someone. Like a psychologist or something."

"I thought about it. What can they do? Tell me to take one day at a time like everyone else does. A hell of a lot of good that will do. No, I don't think anything is ever going to help."

"I know it's hard, Terry. They didn't hurt me as much or for as long as they did you, but I know it's a really hard thing to live with. I was hoping that doing this, something that has real meaning, would help. For me, anything that keeps me busy helps."

"It sort of helps me too. I've done other things, too, that I thought would help. But they only made me feel better for a little while. So no matter what, I won't do them again."

"What did you do that made you feel better even for a little while?"

"If I tell you, will you promise me that you won't ever tell anyone what I did?"

"Of course I will," Lisa said, smiling slightly at how serious Terry was acting. "But whatever it is that you did, it can't be all that serious."

"It is, Lisa, it really is."

"You didn't hurt anyone though, did you?"

Terry sighed, then nodded her head a couple of times. "Yes, I did hurt them."

"Who?"

"Men just like the men who came and raped and beat on us when we couldn't do anything to stop them."

"How did you hurt them?"

"I killed them. They tried to do all the same things to me as those other men did, so I killed them. All three of them."

Even though Lisa was shocked by what she just heard, she tried to remain calm. "Were they the three men who were just murdered?"

"Yes. Three horrible men who won't hurt any more girls like us. I'm not sorry for what I did to them, I just wish it would make me feel better. It doesn't, so I won't ever bother doing it again."

"How," Lisa asked, the doubt and shock echoing in her voice, "could a girl like you kill three men?"

The question made Terry smile. "It was easy actually. Men like that, they're so damn arrogant and stupid that they think they can do whatever they want when they get you alone. If you let them do some things, then make a game out of it, it doesn't take long to find the chance to stick a knife in them. Or grab their precious gun and blow their ugly head off."

"Do you mean that you really did kill them, Terry?"

166

"Yes, I really did. You won't tell anyone, will you?"

"I think I really should, but you're my friend. My best friend now, I think. So I won't tell on you. But you can't ever do it again. Because if you do, then I will have to tell someone what you did."

"You're my best friend too. And you're the only one who knows and understands what it was really like when they made us whores."

"Yes, I do know what it was like to be forced and beaten. We weren't whores. Whores are willing to do it. So please don't ever call yourself or me a whore again."

"I'm sorry, I won't." Terry pointed into the crowd that was now gathered around. "Here comes Jo. I think they're getting ready to go."

She was right; they were in the final stages of their preparations. Dale already had a deputy stationed at each major intersection to direct traffic, ensuring that the cars in the protest had the right of way. And all of those cars drove with their headlights on, just as they would if it were a funeral procession. To start the lineup of cars, Dale first moved his car onto the street, followed by Mack. They moved along slowly, and the deputies directed the other cars, one at a time, to move in behind them.

When they had most of the cars off the high school parking lot and onto the street, one of the deputies radioed Dale that it was time to start moving at a moderate speed.

The rest of the ride to the bridge was uneventful, but that changed radically when they reached the bridge. They had planned to have about half the cars drive across the bridge so that they could spread out the parking on both sides. That way, those farthest away, still wouldn't have too far to walk.

There was no crossing the bridge though. Not with Von Herter and his heavy equipment and more than a dozen armed men blocking their way.

Both Mack and Dale were almost instantly out of their vehicles. They paused for a moment before moving onto the bridge. It was a pause that probably saved their lives. Rich Hayden, the refuge manager, was standing toe to toe with Von Herter, arguing loudly with him.

Their voices were loud enough to carry a huge distance. Not far enough though, for Skip Halbertson to hear. Not that it would have mattered to him even if he had. It was the time he had planned and had waited for. With a shaking hand, he set off the dynamite.

The explosion that followed was a partial success for him. It almost totally destroyed the dam so that part of his plan worked better than he had expected. The part that wasn't successful was his getaway plan. The dynamite proved to be more powerful than he had expected. It did make for a better result as far as the dam was concerned, but it didn't work at all well for him personally. He was way too close to the explosion, and it threw him high into the air. The force of the explosion was so great that he was killed instantly. The only good thing was the fact that he landed far enough away from the now missing dam that his body was found fairly quickly.

CHAPTER 32

Von Herter was sure his plan was working perfectly. There wasn't a damn thing anyone could do now to get on the bridge. Even though Rich was still screaming at him, his eyes lit up when he saw the sheriff's car, followed by Mack Thomas and all the other idiots who thought they could get away with protesting the resort he was heavily invested in.

Then they heard it. Even though it was a few miles away, the sound of the explosion that Skip set off was perfectly clear. And for a few moments, it stopped everything.

Lisa, Jo, and Terry were all furious when they saw what Von Herter was doing. It took both Dale and Mack to hold them back as they struggled to get free and get on the bridge.

Only a few cars back, two teenage boys jumped out of their car and ran for the bridge. With Dale and Mack holding on to the girls, the boys managed to get on the bridge, right where Mack and Dale didn't want them. They knew that under this type of situation, it would be easy for someone to get hurt. And they were so very right in their fear. The danger came quickly, but from something other than the men with guns who were on the bridge.

The first indication that something serious was wrong was when the bridge suddenly vibrated. It felt almost as if it was trembling. Then quickly, it shook hard enough to rattle the metal framework on the upper part of the bridge. Next came a thunderous crashing sound as the surge of water leaving the lake rushed past the bridge with a massive force. The two footings which were too small when they were poured started to give way. That was followed by large cracks in the weakened concrete all through the bridge's structure, which were followed by huge chunks of the concrete breaking loose. That's all it took. The extremely overloaded, poorly constructed, badly designed bridge collapsed.

Von Herter, all his big strong men and their mighty guns, Rich Hayden, and the two teenage boys hit the ice and water at the same time as the millions of dollars of heavy equipment and the bridge itself. Everyone on the bridge was screaming on their way down. Those still alive after it all landed and broke open huge holes in the ice continued to scream for several minutes.

Dale and Mack, along with others, scrambled down what were the original riverbanks to help who and where they could.

Mack immediately noticed someone in the water desperately clinging to the ice still there. It was Eric Von Herter himself. The man with the perfect plan. The man who was behind the destruction and all too often the death of so many people. The man who had done nothing good or decent in his entire life. The man who hated Mack and had made many attempts on his life.

The man who now screamed at Mack.

"Thomas," he yelled as best he could between desperate breaths as he tried to dig his fingers into the ice for a better hold, "you have to get me out of here. This goddamn water is cold."

Mack just stared at him, thinking about whether or not he was going to save the man.

"Thomas, you better get me out or I'll for sure have your ass this time." Von Herter tried to sound tough, but this time, his words came out in a pathetic squeak.

Mack didn't answer. He just stood there, watching Von Herter's hands slowly slip on the ice.

"Damn you to hell, Thomas," he whimpered, "do something. At least say something."

Mack continued to stare at him, then shook his head, and said, "Have a nice swim."

"Why you…" Von Herter said as he slipped the rest of the way into the water, then under the ice.

Mack turned around, looking for someone who had at least some kind of value that might need his help. Instead, Dale was the one who was there.

"You've got to come with me, Mack. It's Rich. He's bad hurt, and he insists that he has to talk to you. Something about Jason and Elaine. We better hurry. I don't think he's going to make it."

Rich was in very bad shape. He was trapped under a huge steel girder right at the shore. It was obvious that the lower half of his body was crushed. He motioned for Mack to come close.

"Mack," he said, his voice barely above a whisper, "That night Mandy died and you fought Jason and Elaine." He paused, trying desperately trying to catch his breath.

Dale sensed that Rich had something very important to say, so he moved in as close to Rich as he could. Too many things had happened around that time which were not fully resolved, and Dale didn't want to miss it if Rich could in any way help solve any part of them.

Rich continued, "I was there, Mack, right at the end. I heard Elaine say she killed Mandy." Rich again gasped for breath, his life obviously ebbing away. "After you left, I killed them, buried them, and got rid of all the evidence. They're both dead. I just wanted you to…" He died then.

Mack had a hard time believing what he just heard. So he was momentarily in shock, shock brought on not only by Rich's words, but by the death of his very good friend. At the same time, it was an unexpected relief to know that it was likely that the man Jason, who was once his best friend, then at the end his worst enemy, was dead. Somewhere in his life, he had gone from a reasonably decent kid to a person who sold his heart and soul for more money. Elaine had been Rich's wife at the time, but she was even more heartless than Jason and had in fact murdered not only Mandy, Mack's fiancée, but several other women.

Mack couldn't dwell on it. It was still possible that there might be more people alive who needed help, so he continued to search the wreckage that had once been a bridge and millions of dollars of construction equipment.

Sirens could be heard in the distance. They were from ambulances on the way for the injured that were found. Even so, lot of people were still searching for anyone needing help. Among the searchers were the three girls who organized the protest.

They were moving along the shore of what had been the lake which was created by building the now demolished dam. Even though the lake was now essentially gone, the original riverbed was still there and deep enough to be dangerous. As they walked, they watched for anything floating by them, just in case it was a person or even a now dead body. They didn't get far though, before Jo made a serious mistake and slipped on a large piece of ice and suddenly was in the water. Terry jumped in after her, managed to get a hold of her arm, and drag her close enough to shore so Lisa could reach her arm and pull her out of the water.

When Terry let Jo go, her now soaking wet, heavy winter clothes, started to drag her down as the river current pulled her away from shore. Lisa screamed her name as she reached out for her, but Terry remained calm.

"Lisa," she managed to say, without trying to take Lisa's hand, "I think it's probably better this way."

With that, she was pulled under a floating junk of ice. Watching it happen, Lisa knew that she would never again see anything so horrifying. She totally broke down and cried so hard her sobs could be heard a fair distance away.

And Mack was within that distance. The instant he heard her, he ran to her side. At first, all he could do was hold her. Then slowly, her tears subsided, and finally she could talk.

"It's Terry," she just barely managed to say. "Jo fell in and she jumped in and got her out. But I couldn't reach her, so she couldn't get out of the water, and she went down under the ice. She's gone, Mack. My best friend is dead."

With that, she started to cry again. Mack stayed with her, holding her, until her crying again slowed, then stopped. She turned her face toward Mack.

"Is all this my fault?" she asked. "It was my idea to get all these people here. It must be my fault that all this happened. All I wanted to do, Mack, is to save the refuge. Just save this refuge. But look what happened."

"I can see what happened," Mack said, as he suddenly realized that all that had happened, all the destruction around them, did have some good to it. Maybe a lot of good. "But, Lisa, along with all the bad things of today, I think there is some good to it too."

"How can you say that? All this is just horrible. Poor Terry. She shouldn't have had to die, just for this."

"I understand how you feel. I lost a good friend today too. Rich Hayden was killed when the bridge came down. And just like you, if I could change it and bring him and Terry back I would. But I can't. So all we can do now, even in our grief for our lost friends, is to continue on."

"I was trying to do that with what was supposed to happen today. And all I did was make things much worse."

"What happened here was a tragedy. But because of what just happened, more was done to save at least part of the refuge than either one of us could have imagined before."

"I still don't see, Mack, how you can talk that way." She pulled away from him as a way of telling him he was all wrong.

"I know you can't, after what's happened. But as far as the refuge is concerned, for now at least, we've gotten most of it back. I think someone must have blown up the dam. That's about the only way all that water could have disappeared. The lake is gone now, along with the dam. This bridge, that I've hated since it was built, is gone. I'll bet that there will be a lot of structural damage to docks and boats and god knows what else. They'll probably be forced to shut the whole resort down. Maybe they'll rebuild it, maybe not. But for now, we do have our refuge back. It's not perfect, but it's a lot better than it was a couple of hours ago."

"Oh, Mack, I'm sorry. I should have known that you knew what you were talking about." She moved into his arms again, hugged him, and said, "I love you, Mack. I love you so much."

Then, having her say those words that way, especially with her being so young and vulnerable, Mack was finally scared. The last thing in the world he ever wanted to do was to hurt her by rejecting her, while at the same time, he knew he couldn't let her get too close. Not that kind of close. He held her anyway, only it was much the same way a brother would hold a younger sister who needed comforting. As soon as he could without making her feel rejected, he let her go.

He took her hand, then also took Jo's hand, who was still sitting on the ground, too shocked to even say anything. Both Lisa and Jo held his hands tightly as he took them back to the road where there were people waiting for someone or something. He found Lisa's father, Bob Anderson, along with Beth, among those closest to the disaster.

He explained to them what happened and left the girls in their care and went looking for Dale. The main thing they needed to do now was to find Terry's father and Jo's parents.

CHAPTER 33

MACK MANAGED THE DIFFICULT TASK of notifying Terry Holstrom's father of her drowning. Her father was, as any good father would be, extremely upset with the news. Mack's assurance the Terry died a hero when she saved other girl's life, helped him get through his initial, overwhelming grief. Mack stayed with him until a good friend of his got there, then returned to the scene of the bridge disaster.

His first question for Dale was "Do we know what caused this yet?"

"We sure do. A kid, Jo Stuart's cousin in fact, blew up the dam. He was killed when the explosion occurred. Since the dam was over in the next county, they'll be handling that part of this mess. We will, of course, be coordinating everything with them. The last thing we need is a lot of duplication of effort, given how much is involved."

"Any idea how many died, Dale?"

"No. Right now, there's no way for an accurate count. Only two of Von Herter's men lived, and they're both in pretty bad shape. Of the rest of those who died, most ended up in the water. So they're floating under the ice, along with Von Herter. Since we don't have the slightest idea of how many of them were there to start, unless the two who lived recover enough to tell us, all we can do is wait for the bodies to turn up before we know."

"Any others besides Rich and Terry killed?"

"Not that we know of. The two teenage boys who got on the bridge were incredibly lucky and only got minor injuries. They landed in water the bridge opened up just ahead of them. Other than that, almost all the losses were Von Herter's men."

"Two dead is two too many, but when you think about how bad it could have been..."

"Mack, you know that there were a lot more than two."

"I'm sorry, Dale. Let me clarify what I meant. There were two deaths that mattered. All the rest who died only matter because their deaths have made our jobs a little easier for a while. Otherwise, they didn't really matter. The only way people like them ever matter is in the harm they do."

Dale shook his head, sighed, then smiled when he said, "I know, but let's try to keep those feelings private. A lot of the public doesn't realize how bad Von Herter and those men on the bridge actually were."

"Yeah, I know. I'll try hard to keep my mouth shut."

"Good."

"What about the bridge? Blowing up the dam is the obvious reason for the water being gone, but what took the bridge down?"

"I don't really know, Mack. I'd bet that the weight of all the construction equipment that Von Herter had parked up there badly overloaded the bridge, but I don't think it was enough to knock it down. I think we'll have to wait until the construction experts finish their investigation of the disaster before we really know why. If they figure it out, that is."

And wait they did. It was weeks before there were any answers for the questions everyone had about the cause of the bridge collapse and the destruction of the dam.

A lot related to the disaster was going on while they waited though. Among the first things were two funerals. Terry Holstrom's body was found fairly quickly, and Rich Hayden's was recovered as they removed the debris from the bridge. Both their funerals were difficult for Mack.

During Terry's service, he sat with Lisa and Beth on either side of him. Lisa held his hand so tightly throughout the service that she nearly stopped its circulation. Beth didn't know Terry but was there for Lisa in case she needed her. Even so, her eyes, like the eyes of most people there, were filled with tears throughout the service.

Rich's funeral was much smaller, but for Mack, nearly as sad as Terry's. He had not only lost a good friend, but someone who both understood Mack's concern about the refuge and the environment in general. He was also Mack's biggest supporter when Mack needed one.

In order to hold his own grief in check, Mack put in as many hours on the job as he could. It wasn't until a few days after the funerals that he took a little time off. And that was only because Rodney Twilabee, the CEO of the company that owned the resort, paid Ben a visit. He called ahead to let Ben know he was coming, so Mack, Roy, and Wanda were all there for the visit.

"I'm not sure," Twilabee said right away, "if this is going to be good or bad news for you, folks. Given all that you've been through since the start of our resort project, I wanted to be the one to tell you what's happening now. As you all know, the dam and bridge disasters have been devastating for our company. Not only is the resort shut down for the foreseeable future, even the price of our stock has dropped considerably."

Roy didn't much like Twilabee, so he couldn't resist commenting on his news that the stock price had dropped. "Turns out, Mack, it was real smart thinking on your part when you sold all that stock." He couldn't help himself then and laughed.

Twilabee did his best to ignore Roy's comment. "To get on with this," he said, "since the resort is shut down, we won't be needing any of the product from the greenhouse now or the gardens next summer. We also know how tight the contract we have with you, Ben, is. So I'm here today to give you a very generous offer to end that contract."

"How generous?" Roy asked.

"Like I said, Roy, very generous." He went over the details with them, which included Ben selling them his townhouse.

"What do all of you think about it?" Ben asked when Twilabee finished.

"I think it's fair," Mack said.

Roy and Wanda agreed with Mack.

"One question," Mack said, "before Dad gives you an answer. What are you planning on doing with the greenhouse?"

"I don't think there is a plan for it. It'll probably just be torn down."

"In that case, can you add the greenhouse and all the related equipment for the greenhouse to the deal? We'll tear it down and haul it away."

"If that will settle the contract, I don't see why not."

"Take the deal, Dad," Mack said, knowing what it would cost to buy the greenhouse new.

Roy and Wanda agreed with Mack.

"Okay," Ben said, "You've got yourself a deal. How soon do I have to move?"

"We aren't going to rush you on that. You can take a couple of months after the contract is signed and settled, if you need them."

After Twilabee left, Roy asked about the greenhouse. "What are your plans for it?"

"Simple," Mack told him, "we are going to hire someone experienced in greenhouse construction, and they are going to take it down and rebuild it at our new ranch. There's plenty enough room there for it and enough land for Dad to vegetable farm however much he wants to."

"I'm going to have to find a place to live though."

"No, Ben, you're not," Roy said "The house at our new place is more than big enough for all of us, and that is especially true given that Wanda and I will be gone part of every year. And while we are gone, it'll be good to know you're there to take care of the place."

"Are you sure about that?" Ben asked. "You know I might be having company now and again."

Roy laughed. "That won't matter a damn, Ben. Theresa's pretty much part of the family now."

"There will be plenty of room," Mack agreed. "I expect I'll be sharing most meals with all of you, but I'm going to move into the guest house. That way, none of my stuff will be in anyone's way."

"It'll be better too," Wanda teased, "when you want to have company, won't it, Mack."

Mack went along with teasing and said, "That is the truth too."

It only took a few days for Lands Magnificent to come up with the new contract for Ben. After a good attorney went over the contract for him, Ben signed it and started the moving process.

Mack had purchased almost all the furnishings in their new home, so they had to go through a sorting-out process as they decided what to keep. A lot of older pieces of Ben's had a lot of memories attached, so they were kept. At the same time, many of the nicer things that came with the place were also kept.

Mack took enough of the castoffs to completely furnish what was originally intended to be a guest house, but what was now his new home.

As things were being settled in for Mack, Ben, Roy, and Wanda, a lot of things in Clayborne County and the town of Kingsburg were rapidly becoming unsettled. One of the larger problems was the pending closing of the only supermarket in Kingsburg.

Mack, though, knew what a good solution would be. So he got together with Kalif Anderson, to implement the solution.

"I know," Mack began, "that our group was organized primarily to get people back on the land. But if we buy the supermarket, as we get more people producing vegetables, meat, eggs, and dairy organically, they will all need an outlet for their products. So I think we should buy Von Herter's supermarket before it closes, to provide a good and fair outlet for those products. We can also turn that store into a lot healthier place for the public to shop."

"The biggest problem with our doing that, Mack," Kalif answered, "is the cost. If we use up that much of our limited funds on the store, there will be a lot of other people we originally wanted to help, out in the cold."

"I knew when I came up with the idea, money would be the biggest problem. So since I think that buying the store will be a huge benefit to everyone involved in our projects, not to mention the employees of the store and the store's customers, I'm prepared to front the initial cost. That is based though, on all the lawyers, accountants, and people in our group who do any of that kind of related work it will take to get the deal done, donate 100 percent of the time they put into it."

Kalif laughed. "I should have known that you would already have a plan to get a project like this moving. Okay, now I agree, we should move ahead on this. How do you want to set up the ownership of the store?"

"Initially at least, I think the organization should retain 51 percent ownership. The other 49 percent should be sold to the employees of the store. Since I'm willing to wait a fairly long time before I'm paid back for the purchase price, I don't think any payments should be made to me the first year. The interest on the money will be minimal so that shouldn't be a problem, and not having to make payments on the purchase price will help the store with any initial cash flow problems."

"What about the store's employees? Are we going to keep the same crew?"

"Most of them, yes. But we will definitely be hiring a new manager. The man in the job now is definitely a typical Von Herter hireling. He is not a nice fellow."

"Do you have someone in mind for the manager, or is that something we'll have to figure out?"

"I do have someone I'd like to make the manager, if she'll take the job. And if she does, I want her salary doubled. If that doesn't fit into the budget, I'll cover part of it until it does fit."

"Okay, Mack, I think we should do it. I assume you want me to take care of all the technical things that need to be done to make this work."

"Because I'm at a total loss as to how to do it, I sure would appreciate it. Besides, since it's your father who runs the bank that foreclosed on the store, it should be easier for the two of you to get through any technical problems. So for right now, the only thing I want to do is to talk to our new manager and tell her about her new job. At the same time, I'm willing to help with any problems that I can."

"All of that's fine with me, Mack. So I think we're good to go on the plan," Kalif said, and they shook hands to settle the deal.

CHAPTER 34

THERE WAS A LOT OF day left when Mack's meeting with Kalif was over, so he decided to pay a visit to the woman he wanted for the new store manager. Audrey Nelson had worked for the store for many years, and Mack had followed her career there since he first met her.

He knew her because her son was one of the boys murdered when he first became a deputy sheriff. She and her husband, in spite of their grief, were among the most cooperative people he had ever worked with. Because of that and the fact that they were simply such decent people, Mack was very fond of them.

Better than that though, Audrey had proven to be very good at her job. She now managed the produce department of the store, which had shown a marked improvement during the time she was in charge of it. And she was able to work into the job of produce manager in spite of the fact that Von Herter hated her.

He fired her after she helped Mack at the time her son was murdered but was forced to rehire her after she filed a discrimination suit against him. She was still doing her job, despite the fact that the store manager was replaced in the last year. The current store manager hated her much the same way Von Herter did. The only reason he didn't fire her was because he knew he'd get sued if he did.

Mack got lucky and found her right away when he went into the store. She was standing next to the lettuce display, stocking it.

He surprised her though, when he walked up to her to say hello. Her first reaction when she saw him was "What happened now? Who got hurt?" And that was a reasonable response. Mack was, after all, a deputy sheriff, and for most people, the only time they had contact with any kind of cop was when something was wrong, when something bad happened.

So even though Mack smiled warmly when he said hello, she immediately answered, "What's wrong, Mack? Who got hurt?"

"No one," Mack said, immediately sorry that he had scared her. "I just came by because I have something I'd like to talk to you about. Something that, I hope anyway, you'll find positive."

"How could I have anything to say that would interest you, Mack? All I do is work in a grocery store. And I won't even be doing that pretty soon, as I assume you know."

"I sure do, Audrey. That's what I want to talk to you about. If you have time, I'd like to do it now. If not, tell me when and where and we'll talk then."

"We can do it now, Mack. I'm due for a break. Is the break room an okay place for you to talk?"

"Sure, if it works for you, it's fine with me."

Once they were settled at small table in the break room with two cups of tepid coffee, Mack started the conversation with what he knew would be a shocking statement and question. "As far as this store closing, it's not going to. It's going to stay open, but under new and very different kind of management."

"How could you know that? Not one person who works here knows anything about the store staying open. All we've been told is that the store is closing because the bank foreclosed on Von Herter's mortgage because he was way behind on the payments. Not to mention all the wholesalers the store owes money to."

"I know because I just left a meeting with the head of the group of investors who will be the new owners."

"Why would you be in a meeting like that? You can't possibly make enough money being a deputy sheriff, at least in this county, to have any left to invest in this store."

"You're right, but I do have enough money to invest. I'd appreciate it though, if you'd not tell anyone that."

"I won't. I still don't know what this has to do with me, other than it's good news the store is staying open, and I might be able to keep my job."

"You have a lot to do with it, Audrey. As soon as the papers are signed and the store is in the hands of the new owners, we want you to take over management of this store."

Audrey's mouth dropped open, and she quickly covered it with her hand. Her eyes were huge with her surprise and the look on her face was something between laughing and crying.

Finally, she said, "Me? Manager? Why? I can't believe any of this."

"We want you, I want you, because I think you have all the qualities it takes to run a store like this. Ever since you and your husband Gus were so helpful after you lost your son, I've sort of paid attention to what you do and how you do things. I'm impressed."

"You have more confidence in me than I do in myself."

"The confidence will come. And a lot quicker than you think. There will be help available too, for any major decisions you need to make that you're not sure of. It's a given that you will make some mistakes, so don't worry about them. Just learn from them and move on."

"I don't know, Mack. It would mean a lot more responsibility. I'm not sure I want to take on all that, especially not for the kind of money I make."

"If I were you," Mack agreed, "I wouldn't either. Not at your current pay. But your new salary will start at double what you now make. After the first three months, you'll be reviewed, and the odds are that at that point, you'll probably get a substantial raise."

"How can you be so sure about all this, Mack? How could you possibly have that kind of influence on something this big and important?"

"Right now, I'd rather not say, but if you take the job, I will tell you why I definitely do have that kind of influence on this whole deal." Mack went on to explain about the group involved and how the ownership was going to be handled.

"So eventually, the employees are going to own the store?"

"Yes. Just as the products the store handles will be improved, a lot of the fresh food will be locally grown and raised, and where possible, prices will be lowered."

"All I can say, Mack," she said, smiling finally, "is that there is no way I could ever turn this offer down. If for some reason I can't cut it as manager, I will have at least tried. If any of this turns out half as good as you say it will, there's no way I could not try."

"That's great, Audrey," Mack said, "I'll let you know—"

Before he could finish what he had to say, the door to the break room was thrown open, then slammed shut. The current store manager stormed into the room, his arm extended with a finger pointed at Audrey.

"Just what the fuck is it that you think you're pulling, bitch?" he screamed. "Breaks are fifteen minutes. You been here more'n thirty-five. I ain't puttin' up with no more a yer bullshit. I'm dockin' yer pay an hour. Now git yer sorry ass back to work. Yer lucky I'm not firin' you."

Mack stood and planted himself a few inches in front of the man.

"Number one," Mack growled at the man, "you will right this instant apologize to Audrey."

"Like hell I will," the man sputtered back.

Mack less than gently took hold of his shirt. "Last chance, apologize or you are the hell out of here. And believe me, you being one of Von Herter's leftovers, there isn't much I'd enjoy today more than hauling *your* sorry ass out of here."

"That there badge don't give you no right to do anything like that."

"I don't need the badge to throw you out of here. Apologize."

Mack smiled, then pushed the manager away. He used his cell phone to call Harley Anderson, the president of the bank that now owned the store. It was a technicality, but Harley did have the authority to fire the manager. Because he'd already been informed of the new deal with the store, which was to the bank's advantage as much as anyone's, he agreed that the manager was now fired and Audrey was already in charge. He also agreed to immediately send someone over to inform all the store employees of that move.

"Well, Audrey," Mack told her with a smile, "your new job has taken effect as of right now, and this clown is all done."

"You can't do that," the man said, his sputtering continuing. "You ain't nothin'. You ain't nobody. So I ain't goin' nowhere. You and this bitch is."

What Mack would have liked to do at that moment is knock the man on his ass. Instead, he laughed.

"Just how do you intend to enforce that order?" Mack asked him. "Call a cop?"

"I'm just going to round up some of the boys here. The bunch of us will show you what enforcin' is about."

"I know that you are actually stupid enough to try that, so go ahead. Just remember, when it's all over, it's you who will be spending at least tonight in a jail cell. Either that or a hospital bed."

"We'll see about that. I'm protecting the store now, so there really ain't a damn thing you can do about it."

Of course he was wrong. While he was out in the store trying to convince other employees to help him throw a deputy sheriff and one of their fellow workers that they all liked out of the store, Mack called for reinforcements. The last thing he wanted to do is get into a physical contest with anyone.

A couple of deputies were there in minutes, and the representative from the bank followed a short time later. It only took a few minutes to get the store keys from the manager and then escort him out of the store.

Mack gave the keys to Audrey and said, "I can only wish you good luck. And tell you that I have no doubts that you can do the job."

"Thank you, Mack. I can't really believe all this yet. And my god, what the hell am I going to tell Gus?"

While the rest of the store's employees lined up to shake Audrey's hand and congratulate her, Mack left the store. He was almost as surprised about the way the day turned out as Audrey, and more than happy about it.

He also hoped that he would never see the ex-manager, Von Herter wannabe again.

CHAPTER 35

MACK NEEDED A BREAK FROM being a cop then, so he decided to go home to see how things were going with Ben's move. Everyone was glad to see him because they were just starting to unload Roy's truck. Most of the furniture had already been moved, so it was almost all boxes this time, and they were very happy to have the extra help. For Mack, it was a welcome diversion from the constant stress of his job. It didn't matter that he loved his job, he still needed a break from it occasionally, as did almost everyone in any part of law enforcement.

That meant unloading boxes from Roy's truck actually felt good. It relieved much of the tension he felt, and he managed to work up a sweat while he stretched some muscles that definitely needed work.

Once the truck was empty, there was enough daylight for a short walk out into Minnesota's bleak winter landscape. So Mack strapped on a pair of snowshoes and headed out to explore a small part of their new farm/ranch. And to Mack, it was a farm and a ranch. The primary purpose of the place was going to be to raise cattle, but now that Ben was living there, it would definitely be a vegetable farm too.

Added to those crops, Mack had plans to raise several laying hens that would be pastured with the cattle as they were moved from pasture to pasture. During the summer months, the cattle would be constantly moved from one small pasture to another, so no part of the land was overgrazed. The length of time in each pasture would depend on the quality of the pasture itself, along with the amount of rainfall.

The chickens that would be moving with the cows would be constantly eating bugs, with bothersome wood ticks and fly larva among the more offensive critters. Chickens also love to constantly scratch the ground for various kinds of food. While they were doing that, they would also be scratching through the cows droppings, where they would not only find even more food, but would also scatter the manure around the pasture. That would cause it to break down faster, so it would quickly become an excellent source of fertilizer rather than something to lay on the ground for a long time and block much needed grass from growing.

Portable coops would be moved along with the chickens into each pasture, to provide a safe nighttime perch for them, and to give them a nesting place to lay their eggs.

Those were only some of the things he hoped to accomplish as soon as the cold Minnesota weather warmed enough. To most people walking out in the snow-covered fields, it would be near impossible to imagine lush green grass growing and a few hundred fat and healthy beef cattle contentedly feeding on it.

Mack didn't have that problem though. As he smoothly moved over the sometimes drifted and always snow-covered ground in his snowshoes, he was seeing the new pastures full of green grass and hungry cows.

As he walked, he saw constant signs of deer, but it wasn't until he reached the river that ran along the boundary of his land that he actually saw any.

It was a small herd of about five, calmly grazing on the other side of the river. Before the dam was blown apart, he could have easily walked across the river on the ice.

Now though, the river was running a lot lower, and the banks were too steep there to climb down. Even if he could, he couldn't have crossed the river. The ice had broken up when the water dropped as fast as it did and landed in sharp, jagged junks over the water.

So the deer continued to ignore him as they fed off the lush browse on their side of the river, while Mack watched and admired their ability to know that he wasn't going to harm them.

He finished his walk through a thick patch of woods, with red oaks being the primary tree that produced large acorn crop. Acorns not only were great browse for deer because they were a primary food source for them, it also made it a great place to watch the fox squirrels scamper around. He made a mental note as he walked, to tell everyone that this place was to be left as it was. No trees would be cut or brush cleared. It wouldn't even be used for pasture.

He knew that in the future, there would be bad times when someone would need healing, and that this small piece of the natural world would be a great place to clear one's head and find answers the human world never provided. It was already tempting him to stop and rest with his back against one of the many large oak trees.

He might have yielded to the temptation if it was earlier in the day. However, it was nearing suppertime, and he wanted to get back before Ben started cooking.

It was a long day for everyone, and Mack wanted to take them all out to save everyone the task of cooking and the cleanup that was always needed at the end of the meal.

No one argued when he got home and suggested eating out, and they all even agreed on the best place to eat.

The Mystic Curve Inn was a recently remodeled bar, located out in the middle of farming country on a two-lane county road. It was one of those places that no one could remember when it wasn't there. So their burgers were fried on an ancient grill that gave them the kind of flavor that would otherwise be impossible to duplicate. Their french fries were just as good, served crispy, and with just right amount of grease on the outside.

It was a pleasant surprise to find Dale and Kathy there when they arrived. They had already ordered their food, but it hadn't been served yet, so they moved enough tables together to make room for all of them.

Two pitchers of beer, with glasses all around, were on the tables. Dale and Kathy had been served their food, and the waitress had just taken everyone's order when eight men walked in.

It was obvious they'd been drinking heavily, and from the sound of their engines when they drove up, everyone in the bar knew that they were snowmobilers. They headed for the bar until one of them stopped and stared at Mack. He was the former manager of Herter's Market.

"Wait a minute now," he said to his friends. "That asshole over there," he pointed at Mack, "he's Mack Thomas. He got me fired today. I'm going to kick his ass."

Dale immediately stood, and at the same time, Roy put his hand on Mack's shoulder so he didn't get up right away.

"There'll be no fighting in here tonight," Dale told the men. "So just calm down, go have your drink, and then be on your way." Dale expected the men to do as he asked because people usually did when the sheriff talked them. These men didn't because he wasn't wearing his uniform, and they were just drunk enough to not realize who Dale was. So all of the eight men laughed.

"Let's kick his ass too," one of the men said.

"No," a different man said, "let's kick all their asses. Then them three pretty ladies can go for a ride with some real men. That'll be a hell of a party for all of us."

Roy could no longer keep Mack sitting down because he was now standing, as were Dale and Ben.

Ben spoke up then. "Okay," he said, knowing that it was highly unlikely anything was going to be settled peaceably, "if you people think you need to kick some ass, we'll give you the chance. But let's take it outside. Emil just remodeled this place, and he doesn't need us busting it up."

"Fine with us," the former store manager said, "we'll take it outside. Be a better place to beat the living hell out of all of you anyway."

"After you," Ben said.

The eight men went out, and Ben, Roy, Dale, and Mack followed. Roy asked Wanda, Theresa, and Kathy to stay inside as he left the table. The eight formed a line and stood more or less paired off, with every intention of making it two to one all around. No one noticed Wanda come out and move behind the man at the end of the line nearest the bar.

Roy got the thing moving. He looked at the two men who were supposed to beat him senseless and laughed. He pointed a finger at them and said, "What do you two pissants plan on doing? You both look like you still suck your momma's tit and piss your pants. And now, you want to fight? What a joke."

They both charged Roy, thinking they were going to totally kick his ass in no time at all. Roy let them get close, with their fists flying, but they had no idea who it was they were going after.

Roy answered their fists with a couple of swift but very smooth moves. It happened so quick that it seemed as though his fists, elbows, knees, and feet all landed at the same time on the two men. It was barely a minute, and both men were on the ground, unconscious. Now there were only five of the somewhat less aggressive men to the attack the four. And there were only five because when Roy made his move, Wanda tapped the man she was behind on the shoulder. When he turned to face her, she hit him with all the strength in her right arm and hand. She was shorter than him, so it hit him as an uppercut. The blow broke his jaw as it snapped his head back. He was unconscious when he landed.

Mack knew it was time then to end it. He moved in on the former manager. He didn't want to hurt his hands, so he hit the man in the gut with a powerful right hand. He gasped and doubled over. Mack was in no mood to play any games, so he grabbed the hair on the back of his head and pulled it down to meet his rapidly rising knee. The man's nose made an audible crunch when it broke. Then he laid down and created a nice pool of blood to lie in.

When Mack looked up, the eight were on the ground, with the three still conscious moaning rather loudly. None of the four had a mark on them. Two more of the men lay at Roy's feet, one at Ben's feet, and one, the biggest of the bunch, at Dale's feet. Wanda was just finishing a strong kick in the guts of the smallest of the bunch of eight that she had knocked down with another strong right hand.

The crowd that had come out of the bar to watch the fight applauded her loudly when her foot landed.

"It's time I think," Dale said, "to call enough deputies to haul all of this bunch to jail."

"Think any of them need to see a doctor?" Ben asked.

"Maybe, but they're all way too dangerous to send them to the hospital. We'll have a doctor come look at them after they're safely locked up. We don't want any innocent people to get hurt."

While Mack and the newly arrived deputies loaded up the now very quiet gang of eight, Dale got the names and numbers of all the bar patrons who witnessed the entire incident.

Once the men were all loaded, it took both Ben and Roy to keep Mack from destroying all the snowmobiles. But he did manage to convince Dale to have them hauled away and locked up. They decided then, to keep them locked up to force all of the men to get a court order to get them back. And that would only happen if they could get past the lawyers Mack would be sure were there to block them. Not to mention that all of the eight men would first have to deal with the numerous assault charges filed against them. So even if they didn't get jail terms, it would cost them a lot to get decent lawyers. As far as beating the charges, there was little chance they could or would, because everyone who was in the bar was ready to testify against them.

Once the eight were hauled into jail, Mack's group went back inside to finish their meal. Dale and Kathy's food had been taken away, and fresh hot meals were being prepared, so everyone was served at the same time. Even the pitchers of beer were replaced to ensure that the beer was cold.

When the meal was finished, the waitress refused to give them the bill.

"Emil," she said, referring to the owner of the bar, "said that after what you did tonight, there would be no way you would be paying for the meal."

"He doesn't have to do that," Mack protested. "If anything, he should be mad at us for being here."

"No, I don't think so. We all know that bunch, and none of us can stand them. They're all bullies. You did all of us a favor tonight, and it was an especially big favor when you forced the fight outside. I, for one, am sorry I missed watching you kick their asses."

With that, Mack agreed to accept the free meal. But he left a hundred dollar tip for the waitresses.

CHAPTER 36

AFTER INCIDENT AT THE BAR, the people anxious to start fights with Mack or any of the deputies were less. Even the normal bar fights were less. For a while anyway.

Crime in general was down too, which gave Mack a little extra time to work with everyone on the ranch. Mack didn't manage to do much of the actual physical work involved, but he was there for all the planning. He also convinced everyone that it would be a good idea to hire Dave Sanders and his brother Paul to do all the carpentry work that was needed. Dave was healing well, so he was now able to do all but the heaviest work. For most of that, they would use other subcontractors.

They also decided to build another house for Wanda and Roy. Everyone wanted Ben to have the big house because it was the best one for every kind of get-togethers, and since he was by far the best cook, it only made sense for him to live there. It added to the reasons for doing it that way when everyone realized that Theresa loved the old house more than anyone else.

So the work moved along as well as any of them expected. Even the new pole barns were up where they would be needed and the greenhouse was up and operational by the time the spring thaw started.

It was an exciting day when the first cattle arrived and were put out to pasture. They felt the pleasure of watching the animals discover their new home, realizing they had all the green grass they could eat and more than enough room to move freely.

The baby chicks arrived a few days later and were immediately at home in the new portable coop that Dave and Paul Sanders built for them. The chicks excited Theresa even more than the cattle did. She requested and was granted the responsibility of their care. It would be a fair amount of work while they were growing, but once they were adult birds, they would need little care. Most of the work involved then would be food and water, collecting their eggs from the nests in the coop every morning, and since they would be running free, finding the nests of eggs left by the hens who decided to lay their eggs outside.

Even before the animals started arriving, Ben's greenhouse was filled with bedding plants for the forty acres he planned to farm, along with many extras for the new organic farmers just starting up. Theresa and Paul Danielson's wife Mary were working for Ben in the greenhouse on a regular basis, and Mary was going to be planting, in her own fields, many of the plants she helped start.

So life was good on, what everyone now simply called the ranch, and for Mack and Wanda, everything improved a great deal. Neither one of them had any bad dreams from the time the bridge went down. Their disappointment though, was the fact they hadn't been able to interpret the dreams ahead of time.

Even so, life on the job was moving along smoothly for Mack. The report on the bridge collapse was completed. It found that the major cause of the disaster was the bad concrete combined with the two footings that were poured too small. The engineers who wrote the report believed the bridge would have eventually collapsed even without all the extra weight from the construction equipment combined with the strong surge of water that came when the dam was blown.

The dam itself was also found to have some construction defects, so it would have eventually failed too.

The cleanup of the bridge and dam sites were nearly completed by spring, and all of the bodies had been recovered. Having the body recovery done was the main thing Lands Magnificent, the company that was responsible for the resort and all of its construction, needed to begin the construction of the new bridge and dam.

Things were different this time though. Rather than hiring out-of-state contractors with questionable reputations, only because they were cheaper, all work was to be done this time by local contractors using local labor.

So even though neither Mack nor anyone else was able to stop the resort from being rebuilt, at least this time it might help the local economy some.

Mack was still upset about not being able to totally stop the resort, but having money now, he had learned a lot about ways to use it for good, rather than just greed. Ben had also learned a lot. So he convinced Mack that the two of them should invest heavily in Lands Magnificent stock while its price was half of what it had been.

Their plan then, was to sell it as soon as it was close to its value before the bridge and dam went down. That way, they could use the money to help salvage the refuge that was still intact and to help more people like Mary Danielson get started in organic farming.

The hope that Mack, Kalif Anderson, and the group they worked with had was to turn a large portion of the land in the area into small independent organic farms of all types.

They also hoped to eventually build the reputation of the area to the point that people from all over Central Minnesota, and maybe even farther away, would be willing to drive to Kingsburg to shop, both in the store they had just bought and the farmer's markets scattered around in many of the nearby towns.

Best of all was the fact that people already farming were selling everything they could produce. Even Ben was having trouble keeping up with the demand for his greenhouse products. He now had Theresa and Mary working full-time and a crew of ten to twelve after-school high school kids working for him. Lisa Anderson was still one of them, and now her friend Jo Stuart was working there too. They all agreed, Ben and employees alike, that the existing greenhouse wasn't big enough, and that they would have to add on more before the next season.

With things moving along so smoothly, it was a shock when a crew cleaning up debris left along the river from the destroyed bridge found two more bodies.

Even though there wasn't much more than bones left, they were quickly identified by the IDs found in the shallow grave that was opened up by the surge of water from the dam disaster. They were Jason Cheman and Elaine Hayden, the two people responsible for so many deaths and other problems that had happened when Mack first returned home from the rodeo circuit.

Mack had had a terrible fight with the two of them the night his fiancée, Mandy, was murdered by Elaine. Mack left them that night, badly beaten, in the refuge where the fight occurred, and went home. Once there, he called Dale Magee, who tried to check out the fight scene and make sure that Jason and Elaine were okay. He didn't find anything because Rich Hayden had arrived near the end of the fight and, when Mack left, had buried the two alive in a shallow grave. He then destroyed all evidence of the fight and removed all the vehicles that were there.

Since it had all happened in the past, Mack and Dale agreed that it would do no good to tell anyone about the confession Rich made just before dying at the bridge disaster. His confession was proof, though, that Mack had nothing to do with their deaths.

Mack was suddenly in trouble anyway. The man who hated him for little to no reason, Assistant District Attorney Ralph Saxton, filed murder charges against Mack very quickly after the bodies were found. He then demanded that Dale arrest him and lock him up immediately.

Dale, however, wasn't about to do that. He even refused to temporarily suspend Mack. When Ralph told the chief of police of city of Kingsburg to arrest Mack, he also refused to do it. Dale had called him to explain the situation, without telling him about Rich, and that was all the chief needed to ignore Ralph. It didn't hurt that the chief, like almost everyone in local law enforcement, hated Ralph Saxton.

To make sure he was protected from any and all moves Ralph might use against him, Mack hired Kalif Anderson to defend him.

That was a good move on Mack's part, given that Kalif was the best defense attorney in Minnesota. The first thing Mack told him was about Rich's dying confession and that Dale had also heard it. When Mack asked Kalif not to use that information unless it was absolutely necessary, Kalif agreed. Mack wanted to use the information only if he was forced to and then in a manner that would embarrass Ralph.

Ralph's biggest problem was getting anyone to take his side and go against Mack. He was disliked and mistrusted by most people who had ever had dealings with him. Added to that, he was considered by many to be one of the last of Von Herter's men.

Even so, he managed to get a pretrial hearing set for Mack. His main witness to convince the judge that Mack should be put on trial for murder was Dale Magee. He failed, however, to ask Dale the right questions before the hearing and was sure that his testimony about what happened the night of the fight between Mack and Elaine and Jason would be enough to schedule a trial. He wasn't aware that Dale held him in total contempt and wasn't about to cooperate much on the witness stand.

Ralph started the questioning with "You were called the night Mack Thomas murdered Elaine Hayden and Jason Cheman, correct?"

Dale didn't wait for Mack's lawyer, Kalif Anderson, to object. He answered immediately, "Mack didn't murder anyone."

"That wasn't the question. The question was, were you there the night of the murders?"

"To start with, you don't even have absolute proof they were murdered. Add to that, I don't know for sure what you mean by being there? Where exactly and when exactly was I supposed to be someplace?"

"Were you or were you not called to investigate the possibility of a murder which took place in the wildlife refuge? A murder that took place in the exact location the bodies were found."

"No, Ralph, I wasn't called to investigate a possible murder."

"You of all people should know the penalty for perjury. We know you were called by someone from the Thomas residence that night. So why are you lying about it now?"

"I'm not lying about it now. And if you accuse me of perjury again, you will be faced with a lawsuit against you. Again, to answer your question, I was not called by anyone from the Thomas household to investigate a murder, possible or otherwise."

Ralph was becoming very frustrated, and it showed. "But you were called that night?"

"I was, but not for anything about a murder. If you would stop trying to frame Mack Thomas and ask the proper questions, I think we could get through this hearing a lot quicker."

"You had better," Ralph said, his voice coming out like a snake's hiss, "be more careful, Sheriff, what you accuse people of."

"I'm not accusing you of anything, Ralph. I was just stating a fact. That fact being that you are trying to frame Mack Thomas for something he definitely did not do."

"What do you think happened then, Sheriff, that those two decent people just buried themselves?"

"Not at all. They weren't decent people either. They were guilty of many crimes, murder among them. I just know without any doubt at all that Mack Thomas did not kill anyone on the night in question. I also know that even if I didn't have that knowledge, you don't have anywhere enough proof of anything to take Mack to trial. With what you have, we shouldn't even be wasting everyone's time with this hearing. This hearing, is in reality, just you trying to frame Mack Thomas."

Ralph lost it then. He turned to the judge and said, "I demand this man be immediately arrested for perjury."

The judge, with a disgusted look on his face, shook his head, then said, "Don't be ridiculous. If you have any more questions, ask them. Otherwise, excuse the witness."

Ralph, his anger showing in his now bright red face, asked, "How can you be so absolutely sure Mack Thomas did not commit those two murders?"

"That's actually quite simple, Ralph. I know who did it."

"Why hasn't that person been arrested then?" Ralph demanded to know.

"He's dead. I can't arrest a dead man."

"That's pretty damn convenient. Once again, I need to remind you of the penalty for perjury."

"And I need to remind you that you can be sued for libel. It's time, Ralph, for you to end this charade. To stop trying to frame Mack. It's my bet that everyone here is very tired of you and what you're trying to do."

"If you know someone other than Mack Thomas is guilty of those murders, I demand that you tell us who it is."

Dale looked at the judge. "Do I have to reveal the man's name, Your Honor? He was a good man, and I really hate to smear his name."

"I'm afraid so," the judge told him. "It's the only way we're going to end this hearing."

Dale shook his head, making it obvious that he didn't want to tell them Rich's name, but knowing he had to, he said, "Rich Hayden. Elaine's husband, Rich Hayden killed them. He then cleaned up the area where the fight occurred. That's why I couldn't find any sign of a fight when I went to check it out that night."

"That's nonsense. Why would he confess? Even if he did it, he was smart enough to know that a confession would put him in prison."

"He was pinned under a beam from the bridge that had just gone down, and he knew he wasn't going to survive, so he did it to give Mack some peace of mind. He knew that Mack always wondered what happened to them."

"How could confessing to you give Mack peace of mind?"

"Mack was there, and we both heard it together. They were Rich's last words. He died immediately after."

"Either that," Ralph accused Dale, "or the two of you killed him too." Ralph was so angry now that he had reached the point of spitting when he talked. He turned to the judge. "I totally demand this time that Dale Magee and Mack Thomas be arrested for the murders of Elaine Hayden, Jason Cheman, and Rich Hayden. They are both guilty. They have to be."

"That's enough," the judge said. "This hearing is over. Everyone can go home now. You though, Ralph Saxton, should seek immediate help for your fragile mental condition."

With that, the judge stood, then left the room.

It was too much for Ralph. In a typical Von Herter fashion, he ran over to one of the deputies guarding the entrance and, before he could be stopped, yanked the gun from the deputy's holster.

The same deputy had quick reflexes though, and before Ralph could point the gun at anyone, he had his arm pinned down toward the ground. Unfortunately, in his deluded state of mind, Ralph did manage to pull the trigger. He shot himself in the foot.

That was enough to take Ralph out of the picture for the foreseeable future. He was taken to the hospital where he was treated for his injury, then when he was sufficiently healed, he was taken to the nearest mental health facility.

No one missed him when he was gone.

CHAPTER 37

MACK TOOK BETH OUT FOR supper, and at Beth's request, they ended the evening at Mack's new home. Beth also made it clear why she wanted to go there. They were in bed right away.

Both of them were hungry, so they made love almost frantically, rested, then made love slowly, taking time to touch and caress each other, getting all they could from every moment.

Some time passed before they talked. Beth was the first to speak.

"I know," she said, "that there's been a lot going on, but it seems like we have less and less time together."

"You're right, we haven't spent anywhere near as much time together lately as we should. I will try hard now to change that. With Von Herter gone, things should ease up for me."

"I'm not doubting that you always try to do the right thing, Mack. That's who you are. The problem is that you do it with everyone. I'm not complaining about it, I just want you to know that I really miss you when you get so busy."

"Believe me, I understand. I often miss you so much it hurts."

"There's one thing I can't help wondering about though. Did you miss me much while you were with Linda? While you were guarding her?"

"Yes, I did, Beth. Very much."

"Good, I want you to miss me." She smiled. "Even when you have other things on your mind."

"I always do. So tell me, how is it with the Anderson family? How is Margaret doing?" he asked, referring to Bob Anderson's wife.

"She's doing better, and I think she's coming home soon."

"That's good news. Are you going to stay with them after she does?"

"I am. I'll be staying there as long as they need me or until I get married. When that will be, Mack, I don't know. You haven't asked me yet."

"It's not that I haven't thought about it."

"Really? What's holding you back?"

"Not how I feel about you, that's for sure."

"What then?"

"My job and the way I deal with it. I keep hoping it'll change. That maybe I can change, at least a little."

"I admit, I don't understand most of the reasons you want to be a deputy sheriff when there are so many other things you could do. Things you could do really well. But whether or not you continue to do what you do, why would that keep you from getting married?"

"Too many things could go wrong. If we were married and things did go wrong, it could leave an awful burden on you. I worry about doing that to you."

Beth couldn't help herself. She laughed. "I think, Mack," she said, "that what you're doing now is putting a totally unnecessary burden on yourself. If the time comes that you decide you want to be married, let me decide what burdens I am or am not willing to take on."

"Okay, I will try. Now that we've maybe settled that, tell me more about how everything is at the Andersons?"

"I'm worried about Lisa. Otherwise, everything is about the way they normally are on a dairy farm where there's always more work to do than a person can do."

When Beth said she was worried about Lisa, Mack sat up in the bed. He had been concerned about her too, but now he was suddenly very worried. "What's going on with Lisa?"

"She's depressed. I don't think she's ever gotten over losing her friend, Terry. She doesn't say much or complain at all. She just isn't her normal, positive self. She's even quieter than she was after she was kidnapped."

"Is there anything I can do that would help?"

Beth sat up too. "Actually, I think there is. The one thing that might help her more than anything is going on a horseback ride with you. She's mentioned that she would like to go riding with you several times."

"Why hasn't she asked me? She knows I enjoy our rides as much as she does."

"She thinks you're too busy. Between your job, your ranch, and working with that group helping new farmers, you really don't have much, if any, free time."

"For Lisa, I'll make the time. Remind me in the morning to call her to set up a time for a ride."

"I'll remind you in the morning to stop in Ben's greenhouse instead. It's Saturday tomorrow, so that's where she'll be."

Mack chuckled. "Now I know I'm working too much. I can't even remember what day it is."

"Yes, you are, Mack. Can you even remember why I'm here? Or have you forgotten what we are all about too?"

"That, Beth," he said, as they both laid down and he moved over her, "is something I'll never forget."

"I can see that now," she said as he made one final move, "oh, yes, I can certainly see that now. For sure!"

Mack was silent in his agreement. His body spoke for him.

CHAPTER 38

THEY HAD A BRIGHT BLUE sky, the temperature was in the mid-seventies, and the air was filled with the perfume of wild apple tree blossoms. Lisa led the way along the narrow path through the wooded land on the river side of the ranch.

Lisa was obviously happy to be out riding with Mack, but she was quieter than normal. Mack knew that something was bothering her, so he asked her about it when they stopped to rest the horses after riding a couple of hours.

"A few things are bothering me, Mack," she told him after he asked. "One thing more than the others. Terry."

"That doesn't surprise me. Losing someone you're close to is always hard. It's especially hard when it's someone so young."

"It wouldn't be bothering me this much if it was just that. It would hurt. It would hurt a lot. But there's a couple of things that she said, that she told me, that are bothering me."

"Do you want to talk about them, Lisa?" Mack asked, trying not to let it show that he was extremely interested in anything Lisa could tell him about Terry. He knew he had to be careful with her emotions, so he told her, "If you don't want to talk, it's okay. We've got a beautiful, near perfect day, and I don't mind if we just sit here quiet and enjoy. I can't think of anything I'd rather be doing more than being out here, horseback riding with you."

"I can think of something I'd rather be out here doing with you than horseback riding."

"What could possibly be better than this?"

"Having you make love to me right here and right now. That would be better."

Her answer stunned Mack. She had never been direct about anything like that before. But she was seventeen now, and in less than a year, she would be considered an adult. That didn't make it okay for Mack though. He felt too protective of her, too concerned about her, to allow anything of that nature happen between them. He wasn't sure it would ever be possible, no matter what her age was.

Lisa understood his reaction to her comment, so rather than let it bother her, she kind of enjoyed shocking him. She also did it to remind him that someday she was determined to marry him. She had been since shortly after she met him.

It took Mack a while, but he finally answered her. "That was not something I expected to hear from you, Lisa. You know that can't happen, with me being so much older than you."

"Our age shouldn't matter, and the truth is, it doesn't matter, Mack. Not now. I'm almost eighteen, and in case you haven't noticed, I've grown up."

He had noticed. Her remark helped him suddenly notice even more. It made him look at her with new eyes. What he suddenly saw next to him wasn't the young girl he'd always thought of her as being. Now, suddenly, she became the young woman she really was. The very beautiful young woman, with all the attributes a perfect body could have. The sudden awareness hit Mack hard, and he knew he had to change the subject.

So he asked her again, "Did you want to talk about Terry?"

Lisa smiled. She knew she had shaken Mack up. It was obvious, in his eyes alone, that he was now seeing her differently. So she let him change the subject.

"If I tell you what she said, do you have to tell anyone else?"

"Not unless it involves a crime with someone else involved. If it does, then I will have to investigate it, and probably that will involve

Dale too. He's the sheriff, and it wouldn't be right for me to go ahead with something and not keep him informed."

"That's the only time you have to tell anyone?"

"Pretty much, yes."

"Okay, I'll tell you. I'm only doing this because it really bothers me, and I need someone to talk to about it."

"I want you to know, Lisa, that having you trust me like this means a lot to me."

"Good. What she told me, Mack, is that she killed those three men who were murdered last winter. She said she did it because she thought it would make her feel better to kill the kind of men that hurt her so bad while she was in that horrible home for girls."

"Did it make her feel better?"

"She said it didn't help at all. She said she wasn't going to kill anyone else because killing them didn't help how she felt. She was messed up awful bad, Mack, from what was done to her."

"It would be hard for it to be any other way, Lisa. What she went through would mess anyone up."

"Are you going to tell Dale about it? What she did was a serious crime."

"To be honest with you, Lisa, we already knew she was the one who committed the murders."

"Why didn't you arrest her then? If you had, then maybe she would still be alive."

"And maybe your friend Jo would be dead. That's the kind of thing there are no answers for. We were planning on picking her up after the protest."

"What are you going to do about it now?"

"Probably nothing. Most people think those men were murdered by some drug dealers because of some sort of argument between the dealers. We'll probably let it end there."

"Good, I'm glad you feel that way, Mack. I think you're doing the right thing."

"I hope so. Enough people have been hurt already. Is there anything else you want to tell me about Terry?"

"Actually, there is. I don't think Terry had to die. When I tried to grab her arm to pull her out of the water, she didn't try very hard to reach out to me. She might have let the water pull her away on purpose."

"Are you sure, Lisa? We often remember accidents differently from the way they happen."

"As sure as I can be. The last thing she said before she went under the water was 'Perhaps it's better this way.' Even if she didn't do it on purpose, I don't think she minded that it was happening. She was in a lot of pain. The worst kind of pain. The kind that's mostly in your head."

"I'm sure you're right about that, Lisa. And the truth is, what happened to her should never happen to anyone. The men she killed were not nice. Personally, I think the world is a better place without them."

"It's terrible, I suppose, to think of some people that way, but I agree with you. The world would be a much better place without people like that. I wish I could understand why there are so many of them."

Mack sighed and shook his head as he tried to hold back the flood of memories that always came with the kind of conversation they were having.

Lisa immediately caught the look on his face. Without another word, she wrapped her arms around him. "I understand, Mack," she said, her voice soft, "you've had more than your share of pain too. There isn't much I can do now to ease it, but the day is coming soon, that I will be able to."

For Mack, the feel of her arms around him told him of another story. It wasn't going to happen that day, and maybe not for a long time, but it would be a new story, and she would be in it.

EPILOGUE

THEY WERE MARRIED AT TRINITY Lutheran Church in Kingsburg, but the reception was held at Ben Thomas's home. Ben skipped the wedding, along with Roy, Wanda, Lisa, and Beth Cheman, to prepare the massive spread of food that was going to be served at the reception.

Mack, very uncomfortable in his suit, was best man for his best friend, Dale Magee. Kathy's bridesmaid was an older woman no one knew very well. She was a good friend of Kathy's parents and now a member of the group Mack belonged to, which was helping people who wanted to be organic farmers.

When Mack was introduced to her, her first name, Elaine, stood out so hard for Mack that he forgot her last name. All was quickly forgiven though, as he learned that there were no similarities between her and the other Elaine he had known in recent years.

Mack smiled when he saw Linda, Kathy's mother, sitting in the front row. To Mack, her beauty was so bright, it was like a beacon that lit up the whole church. It was all he could do to pull his eyes away from her and pay attention to the service, which was mercifully short.

Mack waited after the vows were said and the bride and groom were out of the church before he made his escape out the back way.

He took part in all the traditional stuff that was required of him during the early part of the reception. The clothes he was wearing finally got to him though, and he snuck away from the festivities and went next door to change. The one person who might notice his absence the most, Beth, was wearing a big smile and dancing with Bob Anderson as he left.

It was his plan to quickly change and rejoin the party before he was missed. His plan changed when there was a soft knock on his back door. The person standing there was a big surprise. Not many mothers would leave their daughter's wedding reception, even for a moment. Linda stepped in as soon as he opened the door.

"I know," she said, wrapping her arms around him, "that I shouldn't be here now. But after seeing you at the church and the way you looked at me, I just had to have a moment with you alone." She kissed him then, a couple of times. "I've missed you, Mack. Be sure to take time to dance with me before this day is over. I love you." She kissed him again, then quickly left.

"I wonder why," he said to himself, "life has to be so damn complicated."

It was late in the evening before they both managed to be free to dance, so they danced to three slow songs in a row. Neither Beth nor Lisa noticed, as they had already gone home to do chores.

It was a good day, a day that ended without anything bad happening which required the sheriff or his number one deputy to leave the party.

* * * * *

The first Saturday after Dale and Kathy's wedding, Mack visited Paul and Mary Danielson at their new home. It was a warm day, and Mary served homemade lemonade when he got there.

Then they walked the new fields now filled with organic vegetables. Mack had already visited many other new farms in the area, but this was one of the best-looking farms he had been to.

Seeing this farm, along with so many others, gave Mack a great deal of satisfaction. The money he didn't want, the money Jason had somehow gotten hold of, was now doing some real good.

It was doing good in other ways beyond better, safer, and healthier farms. It was giving people like Paul and Mary a new and better life. And nothing showed that more to Mack than watching them walk the fields holding hands. It was a total contrast to their prior relationship.

It was visits like this that held it together for Mack, that made it possible to see the good the world, even after all the day to day misery he continually saw on the job.

* * * * *

It was late in the afternoon, and Mack, Roy, and Wanda were walking their own fields. It was a mostly quiet walk, with only short conversations about parts of their ranching operation as they were encountered.

It was the kind of day and type of walk that left all three of them with smiles on their faces. So far, everything they hoped to do that they had already tried was going better than expected.

Before the walk was over, Roy said so. "I have to tell you, Mack, I couldn't be more pleased with this whole operation."

"Me too, Mack," Wanda agreed. "I don't see how life could get any better."

"For me," Mack told them, "having you two here most of the time now, is the best part of it."

Roy shook his hand, then gave him a hug, to show Mack that he felt the same.

Wanda, being Wanda, gave him a hug, then a long, long kiss, leaving both her and Mack breathless.

Roy laughed.

* * * * *

To no one's surprise, Ben and Theresa announced their wedding plans a few weeks after Dale and Kathy were married. Both Mack and Roy stood up for Ben, and Linda and Kathy for Theresa. They originally planned a small wedding, but their status in the community had grown to the point that trying to keep it small was hopeless.

They were married in the backyard of Ben's house, while several women were in the kitchen preparing the feast that was to follow. Mack kept his eyes straight ahead during the ceremony because he was afraid to look at Linda. It seemed to him that she was even more beautiful than ever. And when he looked around, there were two other women almost as stunning as Linda. Beth was always beautiful to Mack, even when she had just finished milking nearly a hundred cows. Her clothes might help sometimes, but she didn't need anything fancy to look beautiful.

Lisa was another story. Until very recently, Mack had always looked at her as if she was still a kid. That had changed, and now all he could see was the beautiful woman she was growing up to be.

So for him, it was a day of conflicts. He still firmly believed that his future ahead was with Beth, yet he knew that in some way, both Linda and Lisa would be part of his life. With Linda, he was sure that they would just remain friends in the future. With Lisa, he was as much confused as anything. She was still determined to marry him, and she made no secret that she expected too soon after she turned eighteen, which was less than a year away.

So he spent a fair amount of the afternoon dancing with or talking to at least one, but often two of those three ladies. For him, the strangest part was the way the three of them seemed to totally accept, without any sign of any kind of jealousy, the fact that he was splitting his time with them.

There was a fourth woman there that wanted some of his time too. But his relationship with Wanda was only a friendship, but the kind of friendship a brother and sister might have. If they were lucky enough to have it.

It wasn't until the afternoon wore down, and Beth and Lisa went home to do the evening milking chores that Mack went next door to his small home to change clothes.

It didn't surprise him when, just as had happened at the last wedding, there was a soft knock on his back door. He had just removed his shirt and was about to take off his pants when the knock came. So he wasn't fully dressed when he opened the door.

Linda smiled as she stepped inside.

"I know I probably shouldn't be here," she said, "but I wanted to have a few minutes alone with you. It seems as though being around you gives me feelings so different than anything else in my life, that when I am close to you, there's almost nothing else there. I don't understand it or what or why. I still love my husband. Probably more now than the day we were married. So why you?"

"I know, you give me those feelings too. I think that for you and me, something in the heavens got screwed up. I don't know or understand the what or why either. I think we should have met in a different lifetime. It's too bad that there's nothing we can do about it, but there isn't."

"I know, Mack. It is too bad that there is nothing we can do about that. But right now, we are both here and alone, so there is something we can do about today."

"I wish that was true, but I don't think…"

"That's right," Linda said as she started to unbutton her blouse. "Don't think. Not now."

Mack didn't know what to do. Then their eyes met…

* * * * *

Mack finally made his first visit to the refuge office since Rich died. He asked to see the new manager and was told to go ahead to his office. When Mack walked in, the man made no effort to stand or shake Mack's hand. He simply looked up at Mack, with a look that held the contempt he obviously felt toward him.

"I'll keep this simple, Thomas. I've heard all about you. I don't like what I've heard. You apparently think you have some sort of claim on this refuge. You have none. I will not tolerate any of the crap you were pulling while Rich Hayden was here. This refuge will be managed my way and my way only. If you don't follow the rules, I will have you banned from it permanently. That understood?"

"No, it isn't. Why all the hostility? All I have ever done is…"

"I've heard enough from you. You just proved to me that you are everything I thought you would be. Now get out of my office. You are no longer welcome here. And you damn well better be careful while you are in this refuge, or I will have your ass."

Mack didn't bother trying to talk further with the man. It was very clear who and what he represented. He was, without a doubt, a conservative, and like most of them, he didn't give a damn about anything more than the power he had in his own tiny little world, inside his own tiny little mind. A mind that God had been very conservative with, when he supplied the grey matter for it.

Chances for the remaining refuge being salvaged as it should be were now slim to none. And with the Republicans once again in control in Washington, he knew that it was going to take some time for the climate of do nothing but make the rich richer to change. Even that wouldn't happen unless the American people got smart enough to vote them out of office.

So Mack left the refuge with the feeling that as far as the refuge was concerned, it was going to be difficult to impossible to improve or even maintain what was still there.

His only satisfaction then was his own job and the work he was doing with the new organic farmers in the area. And the fact that with most of them putting a lot of pressure on the refuge management, maybe they had a slight chance to save a part of it. That's what he hoped for now. Simply, to save the refuge.

Lightning Source UK Ltd.
Milton Keynes UK
UKHW010705240520
363742UK00004B/166/J